[handwritten notes] if y... lea... Amazon & Goodreads. Just no spoilers, please much Thanks. :)

Behind Frenemy Lines

Chele Pedersen Smith

[handwritten notes] Are they spy lovers or enemies with benefits? enjoy— ♡ Chele

This is a work of fiction. Names, places such as LINK, and other establishments are created by the author for the purpose of storytelling and are not intended to bear a resemblance to any real places or persons, alive or dead and if so, is entirely coincidental.

However, the mention of existing places, businesses, historical events, movies, and celebrities are real but are used fictitiously. The main storyline and outcome involving a former president are pure fiction and the innovation of the author.

Cover art by: Steven Novak

novakillustrations@gmail.com

ISBN: 1975803809

ISBN-13: 978-1975803803

For Hopeful Romantics Everywhere

Bonus Material: Includes the short story,

"Time Hop," following the conclusion.

Chapter One

Chocolate casualties in heart-shaped boxes collided as she elbowed her way through the crowded deli, reaching for the dispenser at the same time as the handsome stranger. A zap zinged her finger, and she withdrew her hand suddenly. Had the machine malfunctioned or was it the derma-transmitter she'd just embedded near his thumb?

"Ladies first."

"Thank you," she blushed, looking up at his height, embarrassed the reflection in his specs caught her slumming in sweats, while he was freshly spruced in a suit and Old Spice. No fair either that she felt the mesmerizing pull into those Baryshnikov baby blues! Getting lost in that ceil sea, time stood still.

"Allow me." The whir of the receipt reeled her

back in as he retrieved her ticket, then punched his own.

"Ah, my lucky number," she sang, holding up twenty-two, just to say something.

"Michael Jordan's—twenty-three!" He flashed his placeholder with a smile. She must have looked blank because he continued, "Not a basketball fan, I take it."

Her burgundy ponytail flopped like a fish when she shook her head.

He was riveted by an odd scar below the nape of her neck. A cigar burn or bullet wound, he wasn't sure. "C'mon, you're wearing the Wizards! Surely you've heard about the best player of all time—Chicago Bulls, retired, opened steak houses, unretired to play here in the capital. *Space Jam* movie with Bugs Bunny…"

Laughing at all the absurd references, she clutched her tattered tee. "This old thing? I'm not much into sorcery, and I certainly hope he didn't use those bulls for steak. I recently moved here from

Europe."

"Ah, that explains it! I was beginning to think *you* were from outer space."

"Maybe I'll rent it. I'm watching movies to brush up on culture and all your interesting phrases."

"I think you'll like if you're a fan of *Looney Tunes*."

"I think the French skunk is cute. Or… maybe it's because love stinks." Her voice trailed off, and her shy smile practically dented the can of sardines in her basket. She felt off game flirting with him but what choice did she have when he was her latest mark.

"Good one," he hooted, eyeing the swinging Cupids above their heads. "Unless you've been jilted?" She squirmed at his sympathetic scrutiny, so he changed the subject. "Your English is fine, though. Where do you hail from?"

Just then the butcher bellowed her number, lucky indeed.

Chapter Two

He's been gone too long. What the hell was he up to? Galaxy stared into the early May night from her office on the fifteenth floor. It was her favorite part of day when dusk set the sun and the moon clocked in, the twinkling city intensified, blanketing Baltimore in a spellbinding brilliance. Creating the perfect backdrop, it was a welcomed distraction, exactly the kind she needed now. If she focused far enough, she could spot the Washington Monument from her view on Federal Hill. Not the one in D.C. but the original statue commemorated in Mount Vernon.

An interrupting knock made her jump. "Still here?" Lee appeared, four take-out cartons dangling from his hands.

"Yeah, it helps to mull over clues while my mind wanders," she murmured, then glancing at her

Movado bangle, turned from the window. "I guess I lost track of time. Oh, Grace Garden, my favorite! You went all the way to Fort Meade."

"Sure, had an appointment at headquarters and I knew how much you liked it. Basically, the only thing I've learned about you!" *Besides, you'd probably have my head if I didn't.*

"What meeting was this and why didn't I know about it?"

"Oh, nothing you'd be interested in," he assured, slipping the flaps out of the Fold-Paks and dealing out chopsticks.

"Try me," she challenged, prodding him with a wooden skewer.

"Geez, you really hate being left out of the loop, huh? I'll pencil that in as number two on the list." Scratching his thumb, he saw her clench. "No worries," he soothed. "Just an athletics meeting. Boring budget stuff. We have to shell out a few bucks for uniforms this year, so now you know all that I know." Plopping down on the overstuffed chaise, he slurped up a pile of noodles. "So anything leap out at ya from the skyscrapers?"

"Not yet, but you'd be surprised what a genius I am on autopilot." She took a seat at her desk. "I had an inkling you'd stop by."

"Psychic or hungry?"

"Something like that," she smiled, stabbing at her Szechuan crab. "I'm at a dead-end and need to pick your brain."

"Okay but be gentle," he warned, dashing to his office for his desk chair. He was pleased she was finally asking for his help. What was under that concrete exterior, anyway? He'd been trying to figure her out ever since Geoffrey threw them together six weeks ago. Coasting on casters, he rode in on his knees looking more like a skateboarder than a secret agent.

"I've been scouring the internet all afternoon. The only remote possibility of threats is the Peace Expo. Some leaders are in town from the United Nations." Munching on snow peas, she opened a bookmark to show him the web page. She tried hiding a yawn. They had been working late all week, and exhaustion was hijacking her energy.

He grabbed his dinner, then turned around and straddled the seat backward, looking over her shoulder.

"Keep tabs on that, but I think it's retaliation for Bin Laden. I don't see any other reason to threaten the White House, do you?"

Gal tried ignoring the tiny hairs mustering along her vertebrae aroused by his bravado. She rotated her neck, stiff from sitting scrunched over the screen all day.

"Here, you need a shoulder rub?" He set his Chinese carry-out on the filing cabinet, spinning her chair so her back faced him, then began kneading her trapezius.

Even though he was a little too close for comfort, she didn't protest. His thick hands were miracle workers through her cowl-neck cashmere.

"You have a lot of knots, Gal. Stressed?" He

asked the last part in a whisper, close to her ear. She shut her eyes, fond of his warm breath permeating her collar, the only part of him deemed safe there. But stress didn't even scratch the surface. The year ended in such a devastating mess; she was amazed she could even get out of bed.

"It's this business we're in," she covered instead. "It's tricky, not to mention frustrating. We can't tell people the amazing things we do or who we really are." There was more truth to that than even Lee realized. "How do you handle it?"

"I have my ways," he said, trying to sound mysterious, chortling at himself instead. "Well, okay, it's mainly the gym. But it can be fun creating alter egos, don't you think?"

"Maybe I'm having an identity crisis," she sighed. "I haven't been able to get myself together lately. I'd love to escape to a deserted island with a stack of books and a slew of cats."

"Number three—bookworm, and four—crazy cat lady." He pretended to scribble in an imaginary notebook. "We're so close to cracking this case, it'll be over soon, and we can lie in a hammock on the beach. And for the record, you seem nicely put together to me."

"Thanks, I think." Flattered, she began to relax. "Been hitting the gym a lot too. I can't shake the tension, though. Where did you learn how to do this? You could open a practice— Lee Clancy's Fancy Fingers, or something like that. Mmm."

"Why, thank you. That sounds more like a piano service, or maybe a chicken joint." He paused to flex his hands. "I took some classes at The Wellness Center last summer when I went undercover as an acupuncturist. I got into it big time, so I enrolled and took in all they had to teach me. I have my jar of pins in the trunk, if you want, I can—"

"No, that's quite alright," she objected.

"You're all tight again. I was just needling you," he chuckled, poking her with his index fingers. "Sorry, that was bad. So, the smart, brave Galaxy O'Jordan is afraid of shots, is she?"

"Number five," she admitted. "We all have our thing."

"Ah, so you wouldn't want me to prick you, then? Sorry, that was even worse," he muttered, embarrassed.

"Yes, it was," she giggled, tucking a stray section of hair behind her ear. She was feeling so calm; she was putty in his hands. That is until she realized it was his lips roving toward her neck, leaving a tingling trail of goosebumps. Oh no, not her kryptonite! She rose abruptly.

"Everything okay? Was the pressure too hard?"

"A tad. Dial it down, Don Juan!" She paced the room, cataloging her mood. She admired his boldness, was intrigued by it even if it scared her. "Don't get me wrong, it felt nice, maybe too good, you know? But at least buy me a drink first." She softened, shifting her glance.

"Sometimes I come on too strong. I'm sorry, I misread your signals. I seem to be doing a lot of apologizing tonight." He stopped, studying her stance. There was something familiar about it that furrowed his brows. "The last thing I want to do is make you uncomfortable. The number one rule is trust." He scooched his chair over to the cabinet to reclaim his food.

"That's true. Let's try to be more open." She resumed her screen position, trying to get the chills out of her mind. "I don't see how you think we've almost solved the case, though. We haven't the slightest clue to what or where the threat is. I know it sounds cliché, but I think it's an inside job."

"I'm a bug specialist," he announced, winding Lo Mein around his chopsticks like a ball of yarn.

"Insects and Asian medicine, how do you find the time?"

"Eavesdropping devices," he smiled. "If it's internal, we can do some planting. But we probably won't need to. I'll bet the family farm on my theory. It's the only logical explanation."

Why, because you're in on it? The last thing she needed was another arrogant man. She had already rid herself of one, even if it wasn't her choice. "Since when did terrorism ever makes sense?" She twirled her chair rhetorically, twisting her tresses into a bun.

"Tell me something about you. Something deep."

"Besides my needle phobia?" She let go of her burgundy-streaked hair, and it unraveled rapidly, falling where it may around her shoulders.

He watched fascinated. "Yes, something juicy."

"Let's see… my favorite childhood meal is mom's mazuricks. They're these crispy turkey cutlets with cheese things, and they're pretty succulent." Her eyes flashed with mischief as she leaned on the crook of her arm.

"You know I didn't mean food," he grinned. "What are your strengths in the field, surely you have some specialties?" He scooted closer, his breath sweet and inviting despite scallions and soy sauce.

"Lipstick Mace," she whispered, whipping a silver tube from her skirt. Popping the cap, she swiveled the stick and nestled it under his nose, swiping a swatch along the divot as he flinched, holding his breath. "Don't worry, this one's a dud, but you do look pretty." She glided a fresh coat of color on her mouth, sealing it with a smack.

"That's hot," he gulped, surprising her. "I like a woman who can take care of herself." He grazed Gal's lips, luring her in for more.

With the lone illumination glowing from the computer monitor, slightly enhanced by the night lights outside her window, Gal took the bait, her inhibitions slipping away with the refined fuzz of his five o'clock shadow.

He gently guided her out of the chair to his lap.

"We shouldn't—" she began, but her mouth was cut off by his. In the muted light, partial silhouettes played tricks, distorting Lee's features and morphing him into someone completely different. Excited by this phenomenon, she slipped off his glasses, so caught up in desire she didn't mind the way he hushed her, although, for women libbers everywhere, she probably should have. The contrast of his strong hands against the curve of her waist made her five-seven frame feel dainty and feminine.

"I also like taking care of a woman," he murmured, his hands traveling up her soft lavender sweater, cupping her breasts restrained by a lacy purple bra.

She was grateful for the recent shopping spree. Pretty undergarments boosted her self-esteem, but she didn't expect anyone else to get a peek at the goods. Not that it mattered much in the dark.

"Is this a roll of quarters or are you happy to see me?" she quipped, feeling a firm swelling beneath her skirt.

"Medallions and I've wanted you since the second week you got here."

"Not the first?" she teased. They'd been flirting since day one. She thought she noticed his interest but didn't want to count too many chickens. She'd do anything to avoid playing the fool again, but now that it was out there, she was free to pounce. So she did.

"Nice," he gasped, approving of her assertive behavior as she fumbled, unfastening his slacks. "Do you want to do this? Land almighty say yes but it's your choice, I swear!"

Untucking his shirt with a forceful tug, she savagely tore it open, buttons popping off in all directions. *What's come over me?* She never had such a strong urge with anyone before, at least not this soon, not even with the love of her life. Something about Lee ignited a fire she hadn't felt in a long time. Maybe it was just her competitive nature taking over, but was it an ethical way to convince the opposition you were on their side? She made a mental note to check the manual.

Lightly stroking his upper torso, she felt a bit like Goldilocks proclaiming his smattering of chest hair 'just right.' Her hand descended, tracing the defined outline of his six-pack before slipping lower past the snap of his pants. His encouraging groan startled her conscience.

With the cinematic sound of a record needle

dragging across a turntable, she asked the cold shower of all questions. "I take it we have safe precautions?"

"Nope, didn't know this would happen. Sorry. Again."

They slumped back in their chairs disappointed.

"A good spy is always prepared. We should know that."

"That's the Boy Scouts," Lee corrected. "But Damn, I wish we kept a first aid kit."

"Well, probably a good thing we don't. We need to get back to work anyway." Damn was right! A crazy night of meaningless sex would do wonders, but she had to keep her wits sharp. No room for costly mistakes. She clasped her mussed hair into the sort of bun flip she always did, groped for her scarlet specs and smoothed her sweater, trying to regain an ounce of professionalism. Trolling more websites, she sighed, feeling bored and let-down. Politics—some consolation prize!

She snuck a glance at Lee. His head was thrown

back in defeat, squeezing the smiley face stress ball she kept on her desk. *Poor guy, it must be rougher on him.* And then she spied something drooping out of his jacket, half-slung on the back of the chair. The meeting minutes! Surely there was more going on than just softball uniforms. A wicked whim skulked in, swaying Galaxy to use her womanhood to her advantage.

Lee cruised closer, clearing his throat. "Okay, back to work," he surrendered, replacing his frames so he could focus. "Any more possible threats?" The baritone tickled the cilia in her ear, setting off a chain reaction that chilled her spine.

"Yeah... you!" Tugging him by the tufts of his hair, their foreheads touched, contemplating their tabooed predicament. Was it lust doing the negotiating or that mystical moment in the middle of the night when even bad ideas sound good?

There was no denying their mutual attraction, and soon they were at it again. Still, Galaxy needed to strategize her ulterior motive. But how best to divert his attention? The quickest, most effective route was much too personal at this stage in the game, and since she was determined to stick to her guns against Russian roulette, the only option left was to carry-on as they were. Besides, she didn't want to give him the wrong idea, and if she was half the spy she knew she was, it was a feat easily achieved.

Planting kisses down his chest, she extended her arm, trying to reach around for the paper, but the tweed coat slackened, slipping off the chair into a heap on the floor. *Criminy!* She tried maneuvering her foot to the left. Maybe she could step on the sheet and slide it under the desk. But the position was too awkward. She teetered, nearly skidding off and giving herself away.

It wasn't long before their quandary presented itself, like teenagers in the backseat of a car. "We should probably call it a night before we get into trouble," he suggested, tapping her arm.

She dawdled, darting her tongue deep, delaying the departure. How to lift the pocket litter now?

"Gal, I mean it, if we don't stop—" He nudged, lifting her up ASAP.

"I guess it's my turn to apologize," she admitted, hopping off his lap. *Crap, now what?* Her only hope was for him to recline, thwarted again. Surely she could snatch the goods then. She paced the room, looking for the best vantage point.

He stretched out his long legs, rubbing his eyes. "No complaints, I enjoyed it immensely. Just give me a few to cool off."

Gal crawled behind his chair, delicately plucking the paper from the folded fabric. His laminated badge played piggyback, conjuring up an even better plan. *He won't get far without this!* Jamming them into her skirt pocket, the mint-green itinerary crumbled, catching on the sharp clip of the I.D.

He opened his eyes. "Whatcha doing under there?"

"I, I um…" She swept the carpet for a crinkly alibi, the only culprits being a sprinkling of fried rice and a million paperclips until she spotted a menu and two cellophane wrappers under the window, flung in the heat of the moment. "I'm claiming our fortunes," she improvised, stretching to fetch their crunchy destinies.

"I think we already sealed our fate." Beckoning, he reached behind his head. Gal popped up empty-handed, letting his arm hook her waist, spooling her in. She raked her fingers across his chest, resting her lips on his forehead.

"This won't help put out the fire," she reminded when he tilted his chin, their lips meeting upside down. She traced the outline of his jaw, fingering the dimpled crease of his laugh line before sifting through his thick, dark hair.

"I don't mind," he confessed, nibbling her earlobe.

"I think we better quit while we're ahead." Wanting him more than anything, she couldn't risk incriminating herself. The subtle scent of his woodsy deodorant now mixed with musky masculinity didn't help her case.

"I suppose you're right. It *is* getting pretty late," he agreed, gliding upright and putting himself together. "What do you think, too macho?" He modeled, not able to close his shirt.

"All you need is a cheesy mustache," she giggled. "Sorry I ripped the buttons."

"Are you kidding? It was sexy as hell." He couldn't resist slipping into her arms, nuzzling the space between her ear and jaw. Things were getting intense again, and Galaxy was this close to pushing him hard against the wall to complete the final act.

"I better walk you to your car, or we'll be here all night," he offered, not wanting to leave at all.

"Good idea," she murmured, then remembered her task. "Oh, wait. I have to wrap up loose ends. I appreciate your gentleman concern, but you don't have to worry about me."

"Nonsense, it's almost one in the morning. Not safe to walk out alone. You'll be protecting *me!* Besides, we need our sleep. We have that briefing in seven hours."

Well, some of us do. "Yeah, of course. All this will be glaring us in the face soon enough. Thanks for curbing my OCD." Snapping the computer off, she gathered her purse and briefcase. Where the blazes would she shred his badge now? It would have to wait unless she found an open Kinkos.

He escorted Gal to her car, kissing her cheek in the tepid breeze, cupping her chin and skimming her lips. "Thanks for a nice evening. Perhaps we'll have better luck next time. Sweet dreams."

She smiled, slipping into her mulberry Soul. She studied the rear view mirror as he strolled to the end of the lot and climbed into his classic red Mustang. "Figures," she grinned, shaking her head. She relaxed on the headrest, delighted with her deceit. Digging into her pocket to produce his government I.D, she sighed contently, feeling a tad evil. *And scoring the minutes from his secret meeting, Gal, you are on fire!*

She drove off wondering what was up with his disappearance act every Monday afternoon. Her bracelet tracked him but where he went didn't make sense or fit their case. Men think they're so smart. Too bad they're so easily distracted. At the next light, she stopped cold, remembering Lee's words as he bade her goodnight. Did he say better luck *next time?* Something told her he didn't mean research.

Chapter Three

Sliding a tray down the chrome cafeteria counter at LINK, a little-known spin-off of the NSA, the tiers of tapioca made her stomach lurch, reminding her what nearly happened the night before. In the light of day, it seemed horrifyingly stupid. All that to pick his pocket, and it had barely been worth it. The agenda turned out to be nothing more than a softball schedule. At least she wouldn't have to face him today.

The thought made her chuckle until guilt barged in. Maybe it was a federal offense to mess with his job. What if it got her fired? And if not, she couldn't keep him away forever. What if he got mad and requested a partner change? She realized then how much she liked his company. Not just the romantic encounter, she admired his confidence and ease too. Maybe he wasn't so arrogant after all. She felt dreamy

just thinking about his good looks and those hands —
how they had been all over her body. A smitten
school girl with a crush, she knocked over a boat of
fries while maneuvering a chocolate mousse. *Alright,
Universe, I hear you.* She returned the splurge,
reaching for a salad instead. A fit cafeteria lady in her
spry seventies appeared with a mop, used to Gal's
spills.

"I'm going to start charging you," she gruffed,
eyes twinkling.

"Sorry, Francine! It's one of those days," she
sighed, snapping out of the daydream. Fooling
around was totally unprofessional, the angel on her
shoulder reprimanded. What if he reported it as
sexual harassment? She worried for a minute, until
poked by the tiny devil's pitchfork, remembered *he*
had come onto her first. Her nerves unclenched.
Should *she* report it? Or did her lipstick give him the
green light from the get go? Either way, he didn't
seem to mind and to be honest, neither did she. She
vowed not to do that again. This was business, not a

dating service. Yes, it was as simple as that! She would keep her head straight and concentrate on the case.

She relaxed, plucking a bottled water from an ice bin. Suddenly, an eclipse loomed overhead. A towering man had cut in front. Turning, he leaned on the metal surface, facing her.

"Well played, Galaxy. Well played," he grinned, whispering close to her ear.

"Lee? How did—" she stumbled, then stopped. His breath near her ear tingled, and she gulped, partly because of it and partly because of getting caught.

"How did I get into the building today?" he smiled, flipping his I.D. between his fingers. "Maybe you forgot about the ocular scan?" Arching his eyebrows, he emphasized his baby blues.

Those again! *Why does he have to be so handsome?* Galaxy tried to stay strong. And just how did he manage to scrape it out of her secret drawer? She meant to shred it, but the declassified room had been busy all morning. She planned to burn bag it after lunch. His proximity, slight stubble, and light aftershave were just enough to swoon her, so she had to think fast. "I only meant that I found your badge on the floor of my office *last night*," she explained, accentuating the words like a special code. It was hard to come up with a defense when all she wanted to do was kiss him.

"Oh, is that where it was?" he asked, amused, not sure he believed her.

She was barely able to slur, "Yes."

"Silly me, it must've fallen out of my suit after our little rendezvous. Luckily my smoldering eyes and password got me in." He moved in tighter, although there wasn't much room to get any cozier. His lips brushed hers, quickening blood flow to her heart. But he stepped back suddenly and could tell she was disappointed. "Not here."

He tried to pay for lunch, but she wouldn't have it. Instead, she stretched the badge around her neck while the cashier held out the scanner.

"Just trying to be a gentleman," he offered, leaning in. "after *last night.*"

She smiled, her face growing hot as she followed Lee to his office so they could talk in private.

When she set the tray down, she noticed she forgot utensils. "Idiot!" she scolded under her breath, more at herself for falling under his spell and not paying attention. "I guess I don't really need the dressing. I'll just eat with my hands." *Universe: 2, me: 0.*

But Lee, who had the foresight to notice, came prepared. "Wanna fork?"

What was it about this man? His striking appearance was obvious, often hidden behind charcoal frames like a tall glass of chiseled Clark Kent. She liked the way his chestnut hair peppered gray at the temples, giving him an experienced, sort of commanding presence, especially when he wore Armani. But his quiet wit snuck in when you least expected it.

"Thanks, I'll take your tool," she smiled, feeling

brazen. Digging into her salad, she crossed her legs at her ankles in a proper lady-like fashion.

He admired her toned calves in the sensible black heels, wondering how she managed to look professional yet scrumptious at the same time. "Too many people around right now, but I'd love a raincheck." He booked a reservation into her hazel eyes.

She stopped mid-bite, stunned, holding his gaze. "I'll bring the umbrella." Tucking a loose tendril behind her ear, she could feel the heat sneak up her onyx blouse, scurry across the boundaries of the Mandarin collar and splatter her cheeks.

He looked away, taking a swig of Diet Pepsi. He didn't want to reveal his true feelings just yet. His gut told him her heart might not be on board. He wasn't sure what her game was or if she was just doing her job, but he liked the challenge.

"So, what do you think about my latest theory? We never got around to discussing it in depth." She tried navigating to safer ground.

He chewed his sandwich, nodding before swallowing. "Yeah, we got a little off topic, didn't we?"

"About that, I never should have let it—"

"No worries, I'm sure it was just the full moon. The werewolf effect." He tried not to laugh. "Won't happen again."

"Oh, good," she sighed, leaning back. *Bummer…*

"Until next month."

She pitched a piece of produce in his direction. "We're under the gun to solve this, in case you forgot. We can't let distractions slow us down, so we better start interviewing suspects. I say we go over to there and start snooping around."

"Nah, it's not coming from inside. That's too movie blockbuster." He popped the radish into his mouth.

"Too bad you played hooky. You'd be caught up to speed by now on the tip this morning. It backs my theory, the easiest way in."

"I didn't ditch! I didn't have my—" He stopped,

his voice rising in frustration. *What was she up to?* He took a deep breath before continuing. "Regardless, we know Mr. President has made some enemies overseas. I've picked up some phone taps, and I can tell the conversations are Pakistani."

"You speak Urdu," Gal stated in disbelief, letting a cucumber fall from her fork.

"No, well, yeah, maybe just an inadequate amount thanks to the internet but they speak English over there. Only a small percentage still speak Urdu, which I was pretty sure I heard in the background. But wow, good spy details. I'm impressed."

Galaxy was now more suspicious of him than ever. Where and what could he have possibly wired to hear that? She snapped the clamshell container closed on her salad then stood. Leaning over him, she rested her hand on the arm of his chair, her lanyard dangling in his face. "Why are you so surprised, because I'm a woman? I'm trained and educated the same as you."

"No, don't make it a feminine issue," he gulped,

enjoying the view from her blouse. "It's just a rare observance by anyone." Her badge skimmed his nose. "Nice, the bra from last night."

"Good eye," she cracked, stepping backward toward the door. "Good spy details." She fought the urge to bite her lip, trying to conceal the growling hunger whetted the night before, which was more than he could hide. Eyes fixated, she backed out of the room, bumping right into their boss, Geoffrey, who was on his way in.

"Hello, Sir," Gal stammered. How much did he hear? He stepped forward, forcing Galaxy to retreat to her original spot. Lee quickly covered his lap with a napkin, setting the sandwich on top.

"So, how goes the case?"

"Following that suspicion from the inside," Galaxy chimed in, hoping to sound more ambitious than she foolishly felt.

"We have appointments this afternoon at the White House."

Gal shot a stunned glance his way. The nerve! A

moment ago he didn't even believe her angle. Now they were going over there together?

"Good, check it out. I knew you two would make excellent partners. Oh, Lee, better be careful about losing your badge. You never know who might get their hands on it. Good day!" His lanky stature disappeared down the hall.

"How did you know I had an appointment this afternoon?" she demanded, still miffed. "You just told me you didn't think it was an inside job!"

"I got a lucky hunch when I grabbed this," he chuckled, waving the napkin at her. "If you want to be discreet and keep things from your partner, maybe a notepad would do the trick. Or use a PDA or a smartphone like a normal person."

Gal reddened as she read the reminder she had jotted down. "Yeah, I have to get more organized." Stuffing it into her pocket, the crinkling only amplified her incompetence. "I made the appointment in line for lunch. I was going to ask you to join me until you were so sure of your terrorist story. I figured I'd check it out first. But now you know, so…are you coming with?"

"Am I invited nicely?" Lee asked. "I only want to go if I'm wanted."

"Oh, you're wanted all right," Gal assured him. *Probably in more ways than one.*

Chapter Four

Clicking across the checkered beige and white tile, their reflections gleamed as they strolled freely through the stanchion ropes in the East Wing entrance hall. At four o'clock, it was a safe bet school children would've gone home by now and they wouldn't have to dodge field trip lines.

"I can tap in here." Lee's voice and Cuban heels echoed between the pillars.

"Seriously?" Gal laughed. "I love that sound. Do you Riverdance?"

"Not really. I went undercover with a dance troupe once, nearly blowing the operation. I was *that* bad," he winked, giving the room a scan. "So, think there are any secret passages?"

"Maybe, thinking of hiding?"

"No, just heard rumors. Plus would be a great way to eavesdrop or set up bugs."

"Hmmm, good thinking. After we interview, we can look around."

Just then a stout woman with a dark complexion and cropped afro approached them wearing a navy power suit. "I'm Anita Pendleton, Director of Communications. Tom got pulled into a project, so I'll be talking to you."

"Good, good," Gal said, eager to get started.

"Why, because she's a girl?" Lee whispered close.

Galaxy rolled her eyes, jabbing him with her elbow. *He has to stop doing that, especially in the middle of an assignment!*

"Ow, very pointy."

"That's the point," Gal whispered, then turned to their interviewee, who looked a little puzzled. "We're from LINK. I'm Galaxy, and this is Lee."

"Nice to meet you. That's the liaison intelligence network, right?"

Nodding, they shook hands and other pleasantries, following Anita to her office in the West

Wing. Lee swept every corner along the way, trying to spot anything that looked remotely like a catacomb.

"Make yourself comfortable," she invited, as they settled into the plump upholstery. "Forgive me. I'm a little fuzzy. What does your division do, exactly?"

"Well, we lay the groundwork, smoothing ties so all agencies can work together. Avoids a lot of toe-stomping," Lee explained.

"I bet it does," she nodded.

"So, Anita, we've heard inklings that the threats might be someone working here?" Gal jumped in. "I know you and Tom handle what news gets out to the public so maybe you have tips that were not yet broadcast?"

"Well, it is a possibility. We do have a few disgruntled advisors and cabinet members. And of course, Republicans are clashing with Democrats lately, so we wonder if there are any ill plans. It's been a very rough sea around here."

"I'm sure it has. Do you suspect anyone in particular?" Gal inquired.

"Personally, I suspect them all," she quipped, half-joking. "It could be anyone, especially after the Benghazi incident."

"What exactly was the threat?" Lee wanted to know. Galaxy could tell he was still skeptical.

"Well, we received a garbled voicemail threatening to blow up Air Force One. We couldn't decipher the reason behind it, but it was right around the time President Obama attended the Olympics in Sochi to try to make amends with Putin. We think perhaps an organization was stirring up trouble so the countries couldn't unite amicably. Nonetheless, it didn't stop him from traveling, and nothing materialized. We can't help wondering if the two are related."

Gal squirmed, staring at her shoe. "Why wouldn't someone want world peace? What would they gain from the U.S. having rocky ground with Russia?"

"So the threat turned out to be empty?" Lee interjected.

"Good question, Galaxy. One we all are pondering. And yes, Lee, I know the warning seems rather trivial, but we have to treat each one seriously. Would you two like some coffee? I can have some brought in. I know I need a boost during the afternoon slump."

"No thanks, we're good," Gal declined. "Is that the only message you've received? What about anything from Pakistan?" She glanced at Lee. "Is there any fear of retaliation from the Bin Laden capture?"

"Just a minute, Anita. I would love some coffee, thanks. Galaxy misspoke on my behalf."

She called for the hostess service and had a carafe sent in. "Seems I work later and later these days and I need the caffeine." The steward poured them a cup.

"Isn't that the truth?" he agreed with a sip. "Now, about the menacing voicemail. Do you think it's a diversion tactic? And what is your position on the Pakistan notion?"

Anita inhaled her cup of Joe before continuing. "It's possible I suppose. We put the FBI and CIA on alert to cover all our bases. I don't think Russia and Pakistan have a connection, though, not against the United States. I don't see why they would care."

"Except to weaken the allies," Lee murmured slowly, staring into his beverage, ideas swirling with the steam. Then his voice rose stronger as he exclaimed, "Maybe someone here doesn't want Russia and the United States to join forces against other countries. That allows Pakistan more strength and possibly a chance to win Russia on their side. They might want the weakest links possible, and then they strike!" He set his mug down in triumph.

"You might have something there," Gal said thoughtfully. "Anita, does that make sense? Would someone want America to fail?"

"Only just about every terrorist group in existence!" Her belittling snort left a welt.

Lee noticed and swooped in. "Of course, that's a given. But she was referring locally, in-house."

"Well, they're politicians," Anita cracked, "Personally, I suspect them all."

The agents stood and thanked her for the information. "We'll see our way out," Lee promised.

In the West Colonnade, Gal asked Lee what he thought as he tossed back a few Tic-Tacs. "I see a way both our speculations could pan out. It could work hand in hand." Taking hers in emphasis, he started down the hall. Galaxy followed, not having much choice.

"I think the way out is the other way," she suggested, words hanging mid-air. She couldn't help note his hands were thick and masculine, with the perfect amount of hair on his wrist. When she looked up, he was scrutinizing every nook and cranny. "Still set on finding a hideaway?"

"Yeah. Don't you think it would be cool to find one?" He palpitated the wall for indentations.

"You mean as a phantom room bugger, right?"

"Maybe," he smiled. They had made decent progress down the corridor, crossing the lobby back into the East Wing where they ducked inside the Green Room.

"Aha!" He touched a life-sized portrait of George Washington, discovering loose edges. He tapped the top with his fists, flaking off gilded paint chips.

"You're wrecking a priceless piece of art just to find a crawl space?"

Lee gave it a hard shove, and the heavy canvas slid up, revealing a dumbwaiter. They gasped.

"Where do you think it goes?" Gal whispered.

"No clue, but since it's a Washington portrait, I would guess the GW bedroom?"

"Wouldn't it be cool if every painting led to said person's chamber?"

"Very! Not enough bedrooms but let's see for ourselves."

"You're not suggesting we actually ride this thing? Will it hold us both?"

"Only one way to find out..." Lee gestured toward the square compartment. "We're lucky. Looks like the fire hauling kind." He whisked off his suit jacket, spreading it on the floor of the mini elevator, impressing her.

"Did you go to finishing school?" she asked in awe, hopping in and sneezing at the stench.

"Why, yes I did. When you're born and bred in the Lone Star State, they expect you to be well-mannered. So I was a forced teen, but it's served me well. Just don't tell my parents. I hate it when they're right."

"Where's your accent, Cowboy?" Gal was flabbergasted. Her partner couldn't be any more American than a good ol' boy from the heart of Texas.

"It comes out now and then, especially after a few brewskis. I try to sound professional for the job. Plus the folks sent me to a Swiss boarding school for two years. They're big into etiquette too."

"Whoa, you come from *rich* Texans? Did they strike oil?" she teased. "By the way, when you said

GW, I thought you meant George Washington, but maybe you're related to George W. Bush?"

"The father of our country, of course! Why, does W still have a bedroom here?" He grimaced, gathering the pulley cord.

"Maybe...who knows, they might book a weekend here and there to get away from it all." She added her strength to the cables. "You tell me since you're family and all."

Lee laughed. "Not all Texans have Bushes in their family tree. No relation. I swear!"

Squished at the moment, she popped off her pumps, thankful for her gym membership. Good thing Lee was athletic and could bend his six-two physique. They wouldn't have wedged themselves into the confined box otherwise, even if his knees were punching him in the face.

They used all their might to hoist the lift, which seemed to inch along at a snail's pace.

"By the way, I was yanking your chain. George Washington never lived in the White House.

Construction wasn't finished until after his term. Maybe that's why he slept everywhere else."

She gave his hand a light smack as they resumed the repetitious chore.

"Ouch! I got a splinter or something." He picked at the webbing near his thumb. "I think the cords are a bit rusty. I wonder how long since they've used it?"

"Not recent, that's for sure." Gal rubbed her upper arms. "Let me see. I'm pretty good at removing splinters. How far do you think we've gone?"

"Probably as far as my pathetic rope climbing took me in gym class." Lee held his hand out for examination, peering over the opening. With his arm the range of a T-rex, he fished out his cell phone, shining the flashlight feature down the cavity. "Actually, not bad. I think we've made decent progress. I don't see the entrance where we climbed in, but each floor must have an exit, right?"

"I suppose. I've never ridden one of these contraptions before. Shine your light over here so I can see. Ow, I feel like a pretzel." She looked closely at his thumb. *Damn.* Just as she suspected, the cable dislodged the derma-transmitter!

"This is no time to think about food. You should've grabbed a bun from the coffee service," Lee snickered then flinched. "Yikes, did you get it out?"

"Yes, you flicked off a shard of metal, but I got it."

"Thanks, much better." He flexed his thumb. "Actually, it's been there awhile. Whatever it was, it's been bugging me for months."

"Well, you're good as new now." She pocketed the tiny patch, grateful the shadows shrouded her guilt. "So, what was up with that coffee klatch anyway? I just wanted to ask my questions and bluke it. But no, you had to go and have a tea party. I was expecting the Mad Hatter to spring in at any moment." The image made her laugh.

"Hey, I needed a java boost, too. It sounded good."

"I think there's more to it than that," Gal

giggled, trying to control an outburst.

"What's so funny?"

"I think it's the dark. I'm a little claustrophobic, and the air in here is pretty stale. I get giddy from nerves. So fess up, Mister." She jabbed his dense chest, practically denting her finger. *Wow, was he wearing an iron shield or what?* It was such tight quarters; she was practically in his lap.

"Okay, okay, when Anita called for the craft service, I stuck a bug under her desk. It was becoming clear she wasn't going to tell us anything specific."

"She did seem jittery, even without the coffee. Thanks for the rescue back there." The closeness in the constricted space brought back the quivers from the lunch line. They had been playful all afternoon, and it was driving her insane. Loosening his tie, she unbuttoned the top of his shirt, running her hand over his firm pecs.

"No problem. Her rudeness was uncalled for, and she practically threw Hillary under the bus. Did you catch that?" He sounded inebriated. "I'm beginning to think this threat was made up. Sochi Olympics? That's so last summer."

"Yes, I thought she was hinting in that direction. See, inside job! Uh, is this okay, or am I out of line here?"

"You're reading between them just fine." He guided her hand to his bulge. "You gave this to me at lunch."

"I noticed," she admitted. "I'm still ravenous from last night. You worked me up and didn't finish."

"And who's the one that stopped us?"

"I didn't want to, believe me," she muffled between kisses. "But someone had to be responsible."

"I don't know if it's possible, but we can try and continue where we left off." He pinched his pants pocket, extracting a foil-wrapped disc.

"Ah, so you came prepared. Planning this were you?"

"Wishful thinking for whenever."

"About time!" Entangled in passion, they did their best to shuck some clothing free. "Just how should we do this?" Patience was not her virtue, and the limited space offered a challenge.

He clutched her hair clip, partly for clearance and to avoid a gouge in the eye, but mostly because he wanted to grab it all day. Now that he had, it was a shame he couldn't see the effect. Just knowing he had uncoiffed her style into a sexy spill was image enough.

They consumed each other like greedy vultures until an abrupt jolt caused Lee to lose his grip. The packet tumbled over the open side, into the abyss.

Panicked, they held each other. Were they falling? The platform didn't move again.

"Whew, that was scary," Gal exhaled. "Do you think this thing will plummet?"

"I think we're stable. But we lost something important."

"Do you have another?"

"Nope, sorry," he whispered into her hair,

inhaling the coconut scent.

She wanted to cry, hindered again. The universe was relentless. Or maybe it was telling her to stop being so cautious all the time. In life, you're either regretting acts you've done or opportunities missed, and she knew this peculiar predicament would never cross her path again.

"Hell, you only live once!" She threw a wet blanket on sensibility and herself on Lee.

Their bodies agreed full-heartedly. When the last bursting orb faded, they relaxed into each other, pleasantly interlaced. Gal wondered if anyone could hear them. "You were pretty loud there, Monsieur."

"You weren't exactly ladylike yourself, Mademoiselle," he laughed. "But I love it! Sounded like a sports arena. No worries, I think these walls are pretty thick. They were built back in the day."

"Don't they say the White House is haunted? Maybe it's just people fornicating in the walls," she sighed, caressing his chest.

"I'd like to think we're the first." Still riding the

aftershock, he pressed his lips hard against hers, delivering an intense kiss. "That was unbelievable, huh? Definitely the oddest place I've ever fucked."

"Absolutely!" she agreed, then marveled, "You're full of surprises, aren't you? You're like this ordinary guy then, Bam! You turn into this sexy superhero."

"Well," he started to say in mock modesty, just as a sudden quake rocked the cube. The cords unraveled, plunging them into the darkness. Their screams this time were for a different reason.

Chapter Five

"How did he sneak around without Secret Service noticing?" Anita demanded, expecting clear-cut answers.

"They haven't been on top of their game lately, so it's possible. He seems to know his way around the place."

"Well, I don't want Fitzy Baker coming around here anymore. He's not to get what he wants, understand?"

"But what if it's his due? He's been unfairly shut out from his family."

"Are you on his side, Tom?" she asked sharply. The Media Specialist must've shaken his head because he didn't respond. Anita continued, "His parents are dead. There's nothing to give him. He should go to Hyannis, try his luck there. If he even is who he claims to be. There isn't any proof that he ever existed."

"Right…wouldn't you be angry too if that was how you felt all your life?"

In the murkiness, Lee awoke to the shrill, metallic vibrations rattling his surroundings. Machine guns! No, he was enveloped in a quiet, heavy mustiness. How long had he been knocked out? He remembered a jarring jolt, slowly regaining memory of the night's events.

The intercepted fragments emitting from his cellphone tickled his brain before he fully recognized their significance. Feeling around, he brought it up. No, a high heel? Remembering he wasn't alone, he nudged his colleague. "Gal, we got a bite on the bug. Are you alright?" When she didn't respond, he gently shook her then thought better of it. He started worrying. It was his fault they were in this mess. If he hadn't insisted on tagging along or better yet if he hadn't been bent on finding secret passages...

Retrieving his phone tucked in a corner, he clicked on the flashlight and checked for a concussion. He was dazzled by the green specks in her hazel eyes and it prompted him to wonder what it was about his feisty partner he found so irresistible. Of course, brunettes were his type, and he found her attractive, but he admired her strength and confidence too. Still, there was something about her he couldn't quite place. Stirred by the brightness, she started blinking. "Thank God. Are you okay?"

Gal felt disoriented. "Where—where are we...Viktor?" She attempted to stand, then noticed she was caged in, only heightening her fear.

"No, it's Lee. We're in the White House underground, stuck in the walls, remember?" *Who the hell was Viktor?*

The frightening news alarmed her until he illuminated the metal box. "Ooh...yeah, right. My head...." She reached up and touched her forehead. A stiff tendril of hair meshed against her skin. "Is it bleeding?"

Guiding the light in that direction, he inspected the wound. "Maybe a skosh. Still got that napkin?"

Patting her jacket, she reached in, tweezed it

with two fingers and waved it at him.

"Man, this sure has gotten around."

"Not so barbaric now, huh, taking notes on paper," she chuckled as he blotted her cut.

"Yeah, kind of bulky administering first aid with a Blackberry, unless maybe on the Star Trek Enterprise. Are you fine everywhere else?" Dabbing her head, he thought how he teased her for being old school. He wouldn't have known about their meeting otherwise, and he certainly wouldn't have had the chance to plant the wire under Anita's desk.

"I think so. What about you, any damage? Hard to tell when we're so wrapped up. All my limbs are asleep."

"Just a cricked neck, I think. Hey, I always wanted to play dirty Twister," he cracked as they separated body parts, making sure they survived in one piece.

She looked down and noticed her blouse unbuttoned. "Oh no, did we—"

"Pick up any evidence? Yes, in fact, my cell was

tracing something when I woke up." Crestfallen their intimate encounter wasn't memorable, he decided it was best to change the subject. "Something about a fizzy bakery kept fading in and out. Have you heard of it? Do you think it has to do with effervescent bomb-making or something?"

"I was just going to ask if we were the ones who broke this thing but hmm, no, I don't know what it means. A soda factory, maybe?"

"Ah, that's it. They're making threats with Mentos geysers." He grinned at the idea, but Gal didn't get it. "Hey, no worries, okay? I don't think it was entirely our fault the dumbwaiter fell. The pulley was ancient."

"Then adding the weight of two people wasn't insane at all," she mused. "Seriously though, what if we missed some crucial information while we were out?"

"Got it covered. I only spring for high quality." He gestured with the device. "It saves to my voicemail, so we'll never miss a word. Oh, and I disabled GPS, so we can't be traced."

"Truly impressive, Cowboy. So you do think with something besides your Goodfella!" She gave him a playful jab.

"Ow, I see the fall hasn't weakened your elbow any." Rubbing his ribs, he smiled, relieved. "Let's see what we missed."

He pushed play but couldn't get a signal. "That's weird, how did it transmit in the first place?"

"We are way down here. I'm shocked you had cell service at all. So, is there a way out of this death trap? I can't stand being cooped up any longer." She could feel the claustrophobia closing in, the jitters making her chatty. She touched the mortared wall in front of them.

Lee lit up the perimeter. "We're off the cable. At the bottom of a cellar, it appears. Wait…I think if we can squeeze by this tapered space, we'll be running loose in the basement."

"How tapered?" She peered around to follow the light. "Maybe we'll fit."

They unjammed themselves from the dented cubicle and stretched, waiting for the pins and needles to subside. Galaxy stood first. "I'll give it a go." Staggering barefoot and stepping painfully on pebbled bits, she shimmied past the crashed vault, sucking in her breath. If she could just get beyond the area, there was sure to be a way out, maybe a staircase or door hatch. Willing herself to constrict like a cat, she managed to get halfway through the crevice. She pushed, but something was holding her back. She looked down and noticed what. "Damn!"

"What's the matter, dead-end? Something blocking us?"

She sighed, embarrassed, then hollered back, "Yeah....just my...female anatomy. I wonder if Angelina Jolie has this problem when she's raiding tombs."

Lee wrangled free, catching up, handing her heels. "Well, I'm pretty partial to them," he whispered.

Gal felt the familiar chills of his technique and

closed her eyes. Reflecting on their confined tryst hours earlier and the previous night's close call, she wondered why he was so intoxicating. Maybe it was his upbringing of cotillions and Swiss boarding school. Chivalry attracted her. It didn't hurt that he was the total package, but she had to keep her wits sharps if she was to accomplish what she was meant to do.

"Thanks….but they're not helping now," she frowned, back to reality. "Maybe you can think of something, Hombre. That is if you can stop sporting wood long enough to pass through the other side."

She was kidding, but her free hand reached back and discovered the truth. "What the hell, Cowboy? Seriously? Are you on meds or something?"

"Sorry, I can't help it. It's you…"

"Well, how is that going to help us get out of here? No one will find us. We'll be here forever, and no—"

His lips clamped hers, muffling the rant traveling down the path. Her anxiety was closing in, and despite the stench of the damp sublevel, Lee's slight sweat and faint aftershave were a welcomed diversion. He surveyed the area, taking charge of the situation.

"Okay, it looks like we have to smash a few bricks." He chose the largest stone from the rubble, then chipped away to make a bigger gap in their escape plan.

They maneuvered the underground maze. The silence hung thick, and partnered with the darkness, made the space narrowly suffocating. For sanity's sake, Lee kept the conversation going.

"How are you doing?"

"Wrecked, but not bad considering. A little dizzy too. Not sure if it's the bump on my head or being in the dark so long."

"Or hunger? I could eat a steer," Lee confessed. "We missed dinner. Now I wish I grabbed a bun off the coffee service."

"I'd kill for a big burger," Galaxy salivated. "You know those gluttonous monsters you

Americans prize yourselves for finishing?"

"Really? A burger...I thought you only ate veggies." Her segregated reference to their country raised a flag, but he brushed it aside, trading it for more urgent matters.

"Just because I have them at lunch, doesn't mean I only eat bunny food. I love the guy stuff, but it doesn't mean I want a guy gut."

"Hey, now." He patted his mid-section. "I do an extensive workout."

Gal smiled, remembering his six-pack.

They made their way through the rough basement. Every so often there were twists and turns.

"There's supposed to be a bowling alley and a chocolatier down here. So you'd think we'd run into something somewhere." Lee threw his light beam ahead as far as he could, making an arc.

"This is no time for a date," she teased. "But, I wouldn't turn down a box of chocolates!"

"Is that how Viktor woos you?" The question had been burning a hole in his brain ever since he woke her.

Gal stumbled over a few crumbled remnants, nearly twisting her ankle. "What? You know Viktor?"

Lee steadied her by the elbow, bracing himself. "Are you married or seeing someone?"

Amused by his worried jealousy, she shook her head, choking down a lump of humility. "No, I was engaged to him but..." She slid down the wall and sat on a pile of broken bricks.

"Oh crap, he died, didn't he? I'm sorry. I'm a clod for bringing it up." He smacked his head, taking a seat on a nearby heap.

"No, you're not. He's fine, unfortunately. Alive and well as far as I know." Galaxy sighed. "He left. I loved him, and he left. He double-crossed me, actually." She was barely audible, feeling foolish for admitting it aloud, for falling for Vik's games.

"Double-crossed? You mean—"

"I don't get out much," she offered with a sad smile. "We worked together on anti-government missions, and if you must know, not only was he a backstabber, it turned out *he* was married. I wasted so much time on him and invested my heart—for what, for him to leave in the middle of Christmas and hop a flight back to Russia to his little family?" She tossed a chunk of terra cotta.

"Whoa—you hooked up with a Soviet spy?"

"Yeah, silly me. That's what I get, right?"

"No, he's a scumbag. If you want my opinion, you're better off without him."

"Thanks." Their lengthy gaze said more than they were ready to admit. Gal hobbled to her feet. "Well, the way out won't find itself, will it?"

They journeyed on until the flashlight dimmed.

Lee flicked the screen. "Now what? I don't want to kill the battery. How's yours?"

She dug into her suit jacket and switched on a bright light to their relief. "Airplane mode. See, I can be techno, but at least I'm not a nomophobe," she teased. They continued on for a while. "So exactly how do you know Vik, again? I destroyed everything about him, so it's not like there's a paper trail. Are you spying on me when you aren't screwing me?"

"No, it's nothing like that!"

"Yeah, that's it, isn't it?" she nipped, suddenly irritable. "You managed to fish your I.D. out of my secret compartment behind the center drawer! No one knows about it, so how do you?"

"Ah-ha! You *did* steal my badge, I knew it!" He pointed a finger in her direction. "And then you have the nerve to blame me of false motives when you're the one who's a petty thief!" Nicked by betrayal, he stomped off a few feet ahead then called back, "Just so you know, I didn't have to stoop so low to find out about Viktor. You were mumbling his name when you came to."

"Oh…wow, I must have been really out of it if I called you that. I haven't seen him in so long." She followed her words into obscurity, catching up to Lee, reaching out to touch his hand. "I'm sorry for snapping."

"Me too," he muttered, ashamed. "I think we're letting the circumstances get the best of us."

Feeling edgy but relieved, he wasn't ready to extinguish their affair just as it was beginning to smolder.

They took a break on a pile of bricks. "Gal, you had me worried for a second. I thought I had a dueling challenge on my hands, making our actions the last two days really bad." He stroked her hair. "Not to mention messy. And dangerous. That's something I'm against."

"You're against danger?" she chuckled. "Then boy, are you in the wrong line of work! I'm sorry, truly — for everything. I told you I hadn't been myself lately."

"Well, I hope not *everything!*" he nudged. "But sounds like it's still fresh. Are you sure we should be doing, well… this? Maybe it's not the best idea."

"Absolutely! It was over a year ago. I'm tired of dwelling on him. It's a relief to move on. You're good for me." She rested her head on his shoulder, then scooted away. "Unless you're attached?"

"Nope. No one has roped this bronco," he

declared, pulling her close. "We sure wouldn't be here if I was. I don't pin my wash on someone else's line."

"Good!" Their eyes locked. "I mean, that we're both available. Okay, so we need to get out of here! We need food, showers, sleep." Gal stood, brushing off crumbled bits of mortar, ready to plod on.

The trek continued through the old basement. "Oh, FYI, Lee, I did take lasso lessons during an undercover rodeo mission once."

"Cool, I was hoping you had some skills. And just for the record, I didn't snoop through your desk. I got a duplicate badge made. Different serial number and updated retinal scan."

"Well, that's a relief. Thank you."

"But now that I know about your secret compartment, I will."

She gave him a coy shove. "Hey, I guess I just panicked. Vik really messed me up. It's hard to trust anyone, you know?"

Lee put his arm around her. "I get it.

Relationships are complicated, especially in this business." *But just in case, I'm going to watch you like a hawk.*

⁂

The path ran out in front of a door.

"Go ahead, see if it opens," Gal whispered.

"It can't be that easy, right?" Lee turned the antique glass knob, probably breakable if need be. The handle jimmied. "Just as I thought. Do you have a credit card or something?"

"Why, because girls love to shop?" she scoffed, handing him her badge.

He wrapped the lanyard around his hand for a firm grasp, sliding it between the doorjamb. After a satisfying click, Lee opened the creaky door, blowing off cobwebs from inside the frame. His light revealed coarse cement steps. "Well, here goes," he said, taking Gal's hand as they entered the threshold.

"Where do you think it goes?" she whispered.

"The GW bedroom?"

"Very funny."

The narrow staircase spiraled steep, reeking of mildew. Lee suspected Galaxy was on the verge of losing it, so he reached behind, offering his hand. "How ya doing back there?"

"Holding up, thanks!"

Just then the crunchy slip of her shoe flaked off concrete crumbs. "Whoa! I'm okay." She stopped to take a deep breath, kicking off her heels and nursing her ankle. "I keep convincing myself that we're almost there. So, are we? I can't stand much more of this."

"We must be, right? I can't imagine this going on much more. I just want to get out of here. Can you believe we've been in the White House twelve hours?"

Trudging up what seemed like one hundred flights, they finally faced another door.

"Oh please don't be locked," Gal whispered. Lee tried the handle, moving it freely but the door didn't budge. They leaned against it, exhausted and frustrated, thinking of plan B.

"I bet it hasn't been open in so long that it's warped," Lee concluded. "If we just push on it with all our might, we could pop it open."

"What might? I haven't an ounce of strength left," Gal sighed, feeling defeated.

"Well, let's muster what we can. Sometimes people get superhuman power in dire circumstances."

"Oh, right—that's easy for you, Superman!" Taking a deep breath and on the count of three, they rammed into the door as hard as they could. Gal winced with pain, but it worked—the door swung in. "Yay!" their weak cheers triumphed, forcing it further and peeking in.

"It *is* a bedroom!" Gal laughed.

"As long as it's not POTUS' quarters, any other room is fine with me!"

"Wouldn't that be a rude awakening?" They shivered, imagining the imploding chaos of explaining themselves to Secret Service.

Venturing inside, they vaulted across the wide bed. Galaxy sunk into the pillows, partially swathed by lacy curtains flowing out from under a crushed velvet valance.

"I feel like royalty!"

"My spine is very grateful right now. You know, I have new found sympathy for shoving Talon Smythe into that locker in ninth grade," he chuckled, stretching out.

"That doesn't sound very nice," Gal scolded in surprise. "Where's my All-American hero?"

"I don't know about hero," he hooted. "But before I joined the agency, I raised some hell on the ranch. That's how boarding school and I got acquainted. Ha, it was pretty embarrassing being expelled by your own mother, but in my defense, Tal deserved it. He wrapped up 'farm fresh' gifts and played Santa with the neighborhood mailboxes."

"That's terrible," Gal gasped, not sure to laugh or be horrified.

"He had a mean spirit. I'm pretty sure he did time in juvie."

"Wait, your mother had you expelled? That seems extreme. Don't parents usually stick up for their kids?"

"She didn't have a choice, being the high school principal and all."

Gal winced. "Ouch, that would be mortifying. And what about Talon? I wonder how he turned out."

"He's an FBI agent." They laughed at the irony. "We cross path sometimes, on much better terms, which is more than I can say for my gut. We have to find some food or a way out."

Gal propped herself up, looking around the room. "Shine your light. See if there are any signs to tell us where we are."

The roaming beam detected a Victorian décor in goldenrod and deep plum with a painting of Honest Abe anchored between tassel curtains.

"I'll take the Lincoln Bedroom for one hundred,

Alex," she guessed when a spotlight fell on a museum plaque below the portrait.

"I should have known. The bed seems extra-long." An authority on height himself, he spread out like a snow angel. "Funny, Lincoln never slept here."

"Your history is messed up," she snickered.

"Well, he still used the sitting area as an office, and sadly his son died of typhoid fever in this bed."

Gal scrambled off, creeped out.

"I'm sure there's been a revolving door of mattresses since. Plenty of other presidents and guests have camped here." Patting the covers, he coaxed her back in, then whispered, "Wanna do the Abe and Mary?"

"I thought you were hungry?" she scoffed, amused.

"I am," he muffled, nibbling her earlobes.

"Well, how can we do that if they never slept here?" she smiled, cradling her collapsed stomach. "Too bad the dumbwaiter's broken. We could call up for room service."

"Hey, we're not at the Plaza." He swept a stray cobweb from her hair. "And if that thing hadn't hurled, we wouldn't be here, which is all my fault so let me make it up to you. Besides, when will we ever have this chance again?"

"Ha, too late, I already used that reasoning earlier."

"The ticket's transferable for this ride too, you know." He prickled whispers down her neck.

The stimulating chills were arousing, the daring location alluring. If only she felt better. His logic made sense. It was like sneaking out when you're grounded— you might as well make it count. Maybe it was the delirium, but wouldn't it make a great story to tell someday? "Well, it *is* a Presidential Suite," she smiled, straddling his lap. "I'd say it's our patriotic duty."

⁂

They lounged contently, smoothing the bedspread

between them. "I think we just made history," Lee sighed, caressing her arm.

"Oh, is that what you'd call it?" she smiled. "Well, I'm afraid we'll be history if we don't feed our souls with something more substantial." Spotting a plastic map on the small table in the sitting area, she stumbled off the bed, famished. "Fire escape routes. Maybe we can find the exit."

They studied the color-coded maze. "Okay, it's almost six. Breakfast should be in the works. The Prez must be up or close to it if he's in town." Lee creaked the door a smidge to survey the hall.

All appeared still, so they crept out, getting a step in before distant voices forced them to duck inside just in time. Sighing relief, they shared a tender glance.

Their forbidden adventure twinkled Lee's eyes with excitement, and suddenly, Gal felt bad for trying to derail him. He really was a nice guy. What was she doing? *Girl, stick to the plan!* But that was easier said than done. Whenever she vowed to resist his charms, she was never quite resilient enough to ward him off. So what exactly *were* they doing? Was this a real relationship or a work partnership with benefits?

"Good time for that voicemail," Lee suggested. She followed him to the window where the heavy drapes offered an acoustic advantage.

"*...Well, I don't want Fitzy Baker coming around here anymore. He's not to get what he wants, understand?*"

"*But what if it's his due? He's been unfairly shut out from his family.*"

"*Are you on his side, Tom?*" The Media Specialist must've shaken his head because he didn't respond. Anita continued, "*His parents are dead. There's nothing to give him. He should go to Hyannis, try his luck there. If he even is who he claims to be. There isn't any proof that he ever existed...*"

"Fitzy's a name, not a place," Gal gasped.

Chapter Six

The ruby red runner covering the marble floor absorbed their footsteps as they pranced ninja-style to the staircase. Sick from hunger and her injured head, the rectangular overview spiraling three flights gave Galaxy vertigo. She clutched Lee's jacket to keep from keeling, nearly colliding with a white-haired maid carrying up a tray. The steaming aroma of morning brew seeped through their nostrils, summoning them like a charmed snake.

"Oh there you are, thanks," Lee said, pouring two mugs and handing one to Gal. "You're a life saver... Justine!" Scanning her name tag, he gave her a warm wink.

She stared at them in amazement, a bit winded. "Sorry Sir, it took a while longer. The elevator's out." Reining in a snip, she was obviously annoyed at the inconvenience. They tried not to look responsible.

"It's all good," Lee assured, raising his cup.

Gal snatched two bagels off the platter with gratitude. Both parties continued on their way. On their descent into the lobby, Galaxy let out a nervous snort.

"The trick is to act like you own the place," Lee advised, taking an exaggerated bite.

"But what a sight we must be. Do you think she's suspicious?" She devoured the bread. "Is it a coincidence the elevator is out?"

"Probably. The cables can't all be connected. I doubt they still use that old dinosaur. It was bound to conk out, but maybe it had limited range. We should be out of here before she says anything." They reached the first-floor landing and made a beeline for the exit, only to bump into Anita.

"Oh," Gal said. "Good morning."

She gave them a quizzical look. "Good morning, yourselves. Are you okay? You look a little beat up."

"We're fine," Lee assured with a smile. "We tripped over a dog walker crossing the street. Gal bumped her head on a stop sign post." Entertained by the absurdity, he hid his grin behind the mug.

"Oh yeah," Gal remembered, touching her head. "Is it bleeding?"

Anita examined it. "Yes, or at least it was. Do you have an appointment here this morning? It's rather early."

"Yes, we do…" Gal flailed for an answer, looking at Lee.

He decided to throw a name out for a test drive. "With Fitzy Baker."

Anita dropped her clipboard but recovered quickly. "Is he here again?" She sounded irritated, but added, "I mean at the White House today? I wasn't aware he was on the schedule."

"Yes, we got word that he was staying in the Lincoln Bedroom," Gal pitched, figuring this would cover their trail in case they found the room less than perfect.

Anita frowned. "I hadn't heard, but good to know. I have a meeting to prepare. I trust you know your way." She made a hasty exit, shaking her head and mumbling, "Dog walker?" as she continued ahead.

"Yes," Lee called out. "She had five dogs, all big."

When she was out of sight, Gal exhaled, laughing on the verge of collapse.

"Okay, onward," Lee said. "Let's get some fuel down the street, pronto."

They half-jogged, crossing the street, dodging taxicabs along the way. Just outside the Pork Fat Diner, Gal pointed out a curly-haired woman in a hoodie, handling several canines on leashes. She looked like an experienced puppet master. They chuckled as they entered the establishment, falling into a booth, exhausted.

"Yeah," Lee gasped. "I saw her the other day. She had a Saint Bernard, a golden retriever, a Great Dane, a Bernese mountain dog and an Irish wolfhound, I think."

"Genius!" Gal praised, skimming the offerings.

"I could eat the whole works. Ah, colossal cherry blossom French toast! Stuffed with tart cherries and berries. And I'm diving into a double side of bacon for sure." She closed the menu. "She must be ripped with muscles. Managing just one of those dogs would knock me flat on my face."

"What do you mean? You're tough. You handled those pulley cables like a pro....hmmm, what a night, huh?" Lee gulped his coffee. "Sorry, I didn't mean to be a lewd pest earlier. I'm into carpe diem, and it seemed like a lucky coincidence landing there, ya know? I notice that happens a lot when I'm with you. I hope you didn't cave just to shut me up."

"Hey, if I didn't want to, believe me, I wouldn't have. Under healthy conditions I would've jumped *you*," she teased. "You're right, though. We couldn't pass it up. It's been a very serendipitous twelve hours. I just hope you don't think I'm easy." She busied herself rearranging the jellies.

"No way. Are you kidding? I had to work my butt off to convince you." He scanned the choices.

"Besides, I hold you in high regards. Pretty smart too, throwing them off the trail by naming our crime scene."

Gal frowned, shaking a sugar packet. "Thanks but I'm a clunk head! What if they hadn't looked in there for a long time? Now I just led them to it. Like robbing a bank and leaving a trail of money." She put her head in her hands, running her fingers through matted hair.

"No, I think it works. It's just the sleep deprivation talking. But the real question is, what's the big deal with this *Fitzy* guy?" He whispered the name as a large woman with a graying bun moseyed up, poised with pen and notepad. She gave them a strange look.

"Rough night, Lee?" She topped off a round of Joe.

Gal's eyebrow shot up, her chick radar emitting boxing gloves. She zoomed in on her name tag. Exactly how well did Rhonda know him? That's crazy, she thought, reeling in jealousy. She's at least thirty years older and a waitress. The friendly ones got the best tips.

"You don't know the half of it," Lee chuckled. "Rho, this is my partner Gal."

"Nice to meet you, Gail," Rhonda acknowledged, speaking to Lee before Gal could correct her. "Another all-night stakeout? I hope you didn't stuff yourself with doughnuts like those other cops."

Lee patted his abs. "Nope, don't worry. But we are running on fumes. I'm going to tackle the Supreme Court special. And I think Gal was eyeing the cherry blossom colossal?"

She nodded, and Rho wandered away, shaking her head.

"Gail?" she huffed.

"Lousy hearing, nothing personal. And if people don't know our real names, it's not exactly a bad thing."

"How come she know yours then?" She blew on her coffee, hoping the blunt inquiry would quiet the green-eyed monster rattling her cage.

"Been coming here for years. New in town, Rho's the first friend I made, and I'll tell you a little secret."

Gal leaned in, not sure she wanted to hear what he was about to say. After all, she saw *The Graduate.*

"A waitress is a good person to know! I can't count how many times she hooked me up with off-menu specials or after hour splurges. She makes sure I get my veggies, and I don't have to worry about sneeze muffins."

Gal smiled, relieved. No wonder he was so comfortable with Justine earlier. The guy loved food. Maybe her mom was right about that old fashioned notion, the way to a guy's heart and all. If she stuck with him, she'd never go hungry, even though he was the cause of their starvation now. On the other hand, he *has* satiated her other appetite. "Ah, good thinking about the cop cover but aren't diners open around the clock anyway?"

"Mostly. I've practically spent the night here on

some cases, though. Speaking of which, what about ours?" They paused as their breakfast arrived.

"Fitzy sounds like a clown name," Gal managed to answer, cramming custard-coated bread into her cheeks and snatching bacon from his plate. "Or a politician."

"Well, the government *is* a circus," he joked, sopping up oozing egg yolk with his toast. "Hyannis sounds familiar, huh? That's Cape Cod, right?"

"A political scandal, maybe?"

"Possibly." They chewed over the latest evidence.

Gal harpooned a cantaloupe chunk from his fruit cup. "What about President Obama? He might know what's going on. If we could interview him…"

"He can't just throw us a bone off the record. That's why he has a media team." When he saw her disappointment, he added, "I like your thinking, though. Everything would be easier if we could cut to the chase." He glugged the milk Rhonda left him. "Wow, that's the most I've seen you eat."

Galaxy looked down at her empty plate, surprised she had pigged out so easily in front of him. Until she was completely comfortable with someone, especially a guy, food became this awkward, impossible thing she pushed around her plate. Funny how a ravenous appetite quells the self-conscious fear of getting meat stuck in your teeth. No wonder he thought she only pecked at salads. Even her favorite Chinese crab hid in the carton, barely touched. "I inhaled that, didn't I? You didn't do too bad yourself. Aren't you going to eat your grits?"

A few puffs of scrambled eggs and a bowl of mush remained. Lee patted his extended pooch and groaned, "Stuffed. How about you?"

"Bloated. You looked pre-occupied. Did you figure something out?"

He examined his last triangle of toast. "Did you ever notice the velvety goodness that forms from the butter soaking in? Mmm, now that's comfort food!" He peeled off the layer, enjoying one last bite.

"That's what you've been thinking about?" she

hooted. "I thought you were deep in thought about Fitzy."

"Hey, you're not the only who thinks better when your mind wanders."

She shook her head in amusement.

Too full from a hearty meal, they savored the walk back to Lee's car, still parked in a garage, blocks away.

"Okay, it's an hour to the office. I'll call Geoff and tell him we're on a lead. We go home, shower and get a nap. Maybe you should get your head checked out." Lee maneuvered the maze of exit ramps. "You might need a tetanus shot."

"No, I'm sure a hot shower is all I need. Where should we meet?" She didn't want Lee getting any clues without her.

"I know you despise needles, but the dumbwaiter was old and probably rusty. No telling how many microbes were hitching a ride. On the other hand, this case will be easier to solve if you have lockjaw so, hmm never mind."

"Okay, okay, you win. I would hate not to be able to point out your mistakes along the way." They enjoyed the freeway in mutual silence.

"I'll text you if I hear anything," Lee yawned, circling the exit. "But I intend to catch a few Z's first. I'm seeing spots."

"Let's sleep together," she blurted, feeling uneasy.

"Gal, you sex maniac," Lee began in mock shame. "Are you never satisfied?"

"I mean actual sleep." She gave his arm a gentle shove. "Partners need to stick together."

Lee stopped at a red light. "Gal, you can count on me. I'm not your ex. I care about you, and you need rest. It doesn't do us any good if we're delirious. Or wait, I see what's going on. You need me to hold your hand while you get inoculated."

Gal slumped back into the seat. "No, don't be silly, I'll be fine." Was he as loyal as he claimed? She didn't want him out of her sight, but she did need her beauty sleep. "Okay, I'll let it go this once. But if any funny business results from going our separate ways, I'll have your neck. You're not the only one with special skills."

"Ahh, right. Viktor was Russian. Did he teach you his secret moves?"

"No, I have my own arsenal, thank you very much! I'll have you know that I trained in Moscow." Oops, she didn't mean to let that slip! Why did she always have to defend women's lib? Nervously fumbling with his visor, a pair of sunglasses tumbled onto her lap, which she promptly donned. She turned and faced him, giving her best movie star pout.

"Wow, Moscow, huh... So you're Russian too?" This revelation was a bit of a shock, and he was man enough to admit, if anyone asked, that it made him uncomfortable.

"I can make a mean dressing," she joked, softening the mood but Lee didn't laugh. "Well, Ukrainian really, but just half," she rushed to add, downgrading the stigma like she always did. "My dad is Irish, and my mom is Crimean."

Lee gave her a sideways look. "So where's *your* accent?"

"It comes out at family reunions," Gal admitted. "As does clog dancing." They both chuckled at that one.

"You're a mystery woman, Galaxy O'Jordan. Ah, I believe this is your chariot, m'lady! Allow me." Unclicking his seatbelt, he sprinted over to open the passenger door, taking her hand as she rose. "Trust me," he emphasized, kissing the tip of her nose. "We have to part sometime."

"And 'parting is such sweet sorrow.' Is that how it goes, Romeo?" She kissed him softly, then, letting her accent peek through, whispered, "I know you'll be a very good boy."

The trick was to act like she owned him and she got into her car still wearing his shades.

Chapter Seven

Galaxy entered her apartment, whacking her knee and swearing at the antique parcel-gilt and walnut armchair, embroidered with the family crest. Even though her mother was Crimean, her great-grandfather had Soviet roots.

She had never gone this long without sleep, not even co-conspiring with Cousin Ivan's assassination attempt on the Russian president at eighteen. But she was half her age then when all-nighters were no brainers. What risky involvement she realized now. Too bad that mission got mucked. The Soviet leaders had recklessly snatched Ukraine after Germany sunk its hooks in with each war. The country was being bounced around like a child of divorce, leaving precedent for other leaders to gain control. And Putin was even more aggressive about it, barging into the area where her mother grew up. Thankfully family moved out by then, but he had to be stopped!

Gal retrieved a black bag from a rosewood armoire, adorned with pewter and an abalone inlay, another family heirloom. Digging around, she salvaged a sterile syringe pack and a vial of Tetanus.

Holding her sleeve between her teeth, she injected herself. It was true she wasn't fond of needles, but it wasn't the phobia she led Lee to believe. She was an RN, administering vaccines to thousands of children in the poor sections of her country. She could give herself one with her eyes closed.

She started to pop a handful of ibuprofen for her aches but had second thoughts. She didn't want to impede her immune system's ability to make antibodies against the toxoid she just introduced.

She decided to call Geoff just in case Lee hadn't brought him up to speed. She needed to cover her bases, or more importantly, her ass. Lee was a generous lover and a gentleman, but she wasn't sure how he operated as an agent. Maybe he had double-crossing in his blood too.

"Geoffrey, Hi, It's Galaxy. Did Lee tell you that we're on a hot case? Oh good, he did. We were on a stake-out all night, so I'm just freshening up before our next move."

Feeling better about her partner, at least for now, she soothed her muscles under a hot shower. Her shoulder throbbed from the entangled plummeting. Pondering events from the last twenty-four hours, she mumbled the name of their latest clue, "Fitzy Baker," deliberately sounding out each syllable as the warm water cascaded down her face. Whoever he was, he better not get in the way! On the other hand, he was making a great decoy.

Googling him would ease her mind, and she made a mental note to do just that. She cranked the heat and unclipped the nozzle attachment, directing the pulsating jets over specific spots of her body. The eight streams massaged her tendons like tiny digits. Her thoughts drifted to Lee. Now *he* was the one with magic fingers! She would lie down on his massage table in an instant.

Once he was in her mind, she found it was very difficult to get him out. Before she knew it, she wasn't thinking of her sore muscles anymore, but his buffed biceps. He was so charming, so smooth; she told him things she hadn't meant to say. They just flowed out like butter in a chicken Kiev.

Oh well, at least now he knew to take her seriously. The mention of the Lincoln Bedroom wasn't a slip. She wanted to throw Anita on the trail of a break-in at the White House to enhance the fabled threat. Lee's naming Baker was just bonus!

Exhausted, she dried off and donned cozy PJs. Climbing into her Tempur-Pedic bed with the fluffy comforter, she sunk into a marshmallowy slumber. She awoke a few hours later to a chiming text.

"You'll never believe who Fitzy Baker is!"

Lee looked up as Galaxy breezed in. *Why did she have*

to look fantastic? After the last twenty-four hours, he wasn't the only one deciding to keep their partnership professional. He didn't hate the sex at all but was starting to wonder if it was wise. Plus that Russian thing... Still, he wanted to grab the hair clip keeping her twist in place and lay one on her. He meant a kiss, but then a different image popped into his mind.

He cleared his throat to rid the inappropriate thought. "You clean up nice."

"Well, the bar is set pretty low after last night. But thanks," she smiled, setting her briefcase on his desk before taking a seat. "You don't scrub up too bad yourself. I meant to search Baker earlier, but I fell asleep. Did you get some rest? Surely you didn't drive back and forth from D.C.?"

"Hell no. I took a shower at the gym downstairs and had a good power nap here on the lounge chair. Did you have time to get that shot?" He looked up from typing as she revealed the Wonder Woman Band-Aid on her arm. "Good deal. Wait a second; it's not just a cover-up, is it?"

"Scout's honor." She peeled back half the adhesive, unveiling the injection site.

"I'm proud of you. I'm glad you won't be just a silent partner."

His praise irked her, making her feel ten years old. It took all her might and a deep breath not to snap. "Look, I'm not petrified of needles, okay? They're just not my favorite thing. So, what did you find out?" She scooted close to his computer, then having second thoughts, backed away.

"I won't bite," he laughed, pushing the laptop near her.

"Yes, you do," she chuckled. "Isn't it how it all began?"

"But it's office hours. The door is wide open, so you're safe. Geoffrey could walk in any minute."

The risk sent a tempting shiver down her spine. No, no more, she scolded her inner sex fiend. "So, Fitzy Baker..." she directed to stay on topic.

"Ah, yes. You know Marilyn Monroe?" Lee

asked, excited about his latest discovery. He was bounding with energy, so he sprang up and shut the door to keep his findings under wraps. This could be their all big exclusive.

"Not personally. You mean the actress in the flowing, white dress over an air grate? I thought she was dead, a long time ago, in fact. What does she have to do with it?"

"She has a big role in this, actually. I don't know when you came to the states, but do you know anything about her history or her affair with a certain president?"

"Not really, it was before my time. I've heard of Bill and Monica though."

"Before mine too, but you hear things. We have these rumor rags called tabloids," he cracked. "Kennedy was well-liked by his constituents, especially by one blonde Hollywood bombshell that got her hooks into him. They were a hot item briefly in the '60s. In fact, there were rumors of a secret tunnel in the White House to sneak her in." Their intimate glance gave rise to goosebumps, realizing they trudged the very path that morning.

Lee clicked on YouTube for the sultry footage of Marilyn singing, "Happy Birthday Mr. President."

"Very nice, a little pitchy but I'm confused. How does this tell us who Fitz Baker is?"

"I'm sure Jack wasn't eyeing her voice if you know what I mean," he winked. "Anyway, I read she fell hard, threatened to go public, so it was a quick ditch to a mental hospital. He had too much to lose, so he pretty much swept her under the rug. She already had an unstable personality."

"I'm guessing dumping her didn't help her state of mind?" Gal empathized, crossing her arms and legs. "Did she plot revenge? Have herself frozen and come back as Fitz Baker to ruin the democracy?" She snorted at the ridiculous thought.

"Almost." Lee eyed her shapely calves and fought the urge to touch her silky stockings. He guzzled his sports bottle to cool off.

Gal leaned forward in shock. "What did she

do?" When she braced her elbows on the desk, Lee noticed her burgundy blouse puckering between the buttons. He tried diverting his attention, but the ends of her paisley scarf drew him in, giving him a bouncy peek. He looked away, but it was too late.

Wheeling his chair as close to the desk as possible, he cleared his throat and continued, hoping to sound sober. "There was some speculation she was pregnant, thus the hiatus. But there were talks of a loss, and when Marilyn was eventually released, a turbulence of depression, pills and alcohol consumed her life until she died."

"How sad! If she lived in this century, she could've run her own life. Early society has been so oppressive." She didn't mean to sound bitter, but she hated when women were forced to be submissive. She thought of her country, her mother, and especially third world areas. "But back to the clue...I still don't see where Fitzy fits in."

"He wasn't the miscarriage after all..."

Gal gasped, "You mean—"

"Yep!" Lee closed the laptop.

"How did you connect him to his famous parents? His last name isn't Kennedy or Monroe."

"Well, Anita's mention of Hyannis kept running through my mind, and then your guess of a scandal melded it all together while I slept—Kennedy territory and one of the juiciest presidential disgraces of all! They went to great lengths to hide it from the media and Jacqueline, of course." He paused to take another swig. "Mind you; this is all just speculation so I'm not sure of the details, or if it's even true, whether Marilyn named him or even saw him after she gave birth—if she gave birth at all."

"This is pretty wild. Do you think anyone will believe it?"

"I don't know. Mind boggling, right? I've been digging deep for over an hour, and there isn't much to go on, not from reliable sources anyway. From what I could gather, Marilyn may have convinced the doctor to let her keep the baby full term. Maybe someone in her family kept him, or she gave him up for adoption. The mental ward could've been a diversion to hide the pregnancy."

Galaxy skimmed through the printouts on his desk. "So a legacy of JFK and Marilyn Monroe lives on. Interesting…"

"Of course, that's it!" Lee, in the middle of a Eureka moment, grasped her shoulders in a congratulatory manner, causing Gal to jump, sending a mass of papers flying. "Sorry to startle you. It's just that I've been racking my brain for this last piece of the puzzle. It's been giving me a headache."

"Well, thanks. Now I have one. Out with it then!" Frowning, she rubbed the upper end of her sore collarbone. Leaning forward again, all ears, she tucked a strand of hair behind one before resting her chin in her hands.

"JFK… his initials were glaring me in the face this whole time, but somehow I overlooked the obvious, his middle name…duh. Fitzgerald!" He tried not to gawk at her blouse.

"Ah, Fitzy," Gal nodded. "So Baker is his

adopted name?"

"Probably. Now to get an actual interview. How do we get to him?" He stretched out in his chair, hands behind his head.

Gal stood, pacing the room. Was it her imagination or was there a pup tent in his pants? Covering her blushing curiosity, she stooped to gather the scattered documents— printed versions of the web pages Lee was researching all afternoon. Organizing the stack, her eye fell on a paragraph as she straightened. "Baker *is* his real name." Glad to finally contribute, she proudly held out the paper for him to see. "It's his mother's."

Lee took the sheet. "Norma Jean Baker. Right, I've heard that before. Duh, again!"

"Fitzy Baker. That's clever," she marveled. "Do you think he was born with it or did he take it on as an adult?"

"I don't know. Maybe it's just dumb luck."

"We can ask Anita how to get in touch with him," Galaxy suggested, coiling a piece of hair for ideas.

"But she thinks we already talked to him, remember?" He drummed his fingers on the desk.

"We can pretend he stood us up. We can say he contacted us, but we don't know how to reach him."

"Hmm, that works. I'll give her a call." Picking up his desk phone, he spotted his cell lighting up like a pinball machine. "Whoa, something's going on." He magnified the sound so they both could hear. The transmission carried some static, so they had to listen carefully, heads close together. The warm exchange of breath brought back the excitement of that first night.

"Make sure all extra bedrooms are locked tight," Anita ordered.

A woman answered, "Yes, ma'am, they have been."

"Well, I don't understand how Fitz got into the Lincoln Bedroom, or how he arranged to meet with LINK. This is getting out of hand."

A man cut in. "That particular bedroom has a back door to the cellar. It's been there since the prohibition because I heard Harding used it to sneak in his booze and it's likely JFK found it handy as well."

"I asked you to blockade all doors, didn't I?" she *barked.*

"I did, Anita. I painted it shut—"

"Well, Tom, do you think that was strong enough? He's in and out like a mouse."

"Ma'am, the little elevator's missing if you find that relevant," the woman volunteered, timidly.

Galaxy and Lee exchanged guilty looks.

The sound of pouring liquid and clinking china clued them into Anita's four o'clock coffee service.

"Do you think that's our girl, Justine?"

Gal shrugged. "Anita's dishing it out to poor Tom, though. I feel bad for him. It's our fault."

"He's a big boy with a high-pressure job. He can take it. Shh, what'd they just say?"

"—but that's a fire hazard," Tom protested.

"I don't care; this is a national security issue. Arrange a search party and find that carrier. Whatever floor it's on, must be where he's staying. And Tom..."

"Yes?" he asked, fed up.

"Cement the doorway this time. We need everything fortified."

A shuffle of feet scurried out, and the door closed with a thud.

"Well, that will keep them busy," Galaxy decided. "I hope we didn't leave any evidence behind." A wistful expression in her eyes met his.

"They're going to find it smashed to smithereens," Lee chuckled. "I think we're good." Craving her irresistible lips, he made a move and took them.

The sound of the door creaking scooted them apart. Geoffrey! If he caught them canoodling...

They scurried, trying to appear busy but when they looked up, no one was there. With blood pressure descending, they sighed relief, realizing it was just Anita back in her office.

Her chair cushion squeaked, expelling air from the weight of its recipient whose sudden snatching of the handset rattled them. "Hey, she wants the place scoured with a fine tooth comb," the hoarse voice informed, surprising them more. "Yeah, no shoe Cinderella, don't you think I know what that means? And more bad news, Smitty, the dumbwaiter's out. So we gotta go with the backup plan." The jarring ring of the slammed receiver signaled a frustrating setback.

"Who was that?" Gal asked, bewildered. "Why was he using Anita's office?"

"I think it's Tom, trying to whisper," Lee laughed.

"I don't know, didn't sound the same. And who do you think Smitty is, some contractor hired to cement the door?"

"Maybe. I wonder if they'll fill in the whole stairwell."

"Hey, what if it's that Fitzy guy?"

"Creeping around in broad sight? I doubt it. Maybe on the other end, though. Whoever it is, they're up to something."

"Ah ha, an inside job!" Gal rejoiced. "You didn't believe me, but it's quite common."

"Yeah, looks like you're right. Good deducing, Sherlock."

She glared for a second, expecting sarcasm, but found genuine approval instead. "Thanks," she smiled, surprised at his forfeit. Lee's stare of admiration unnerved her, so she broke contact, her eyes falling on the print pile instead. "Poor Fitz, it must be awful for him, being tossed aside and kept from his legacy."

"Yeah, but we haven't met him yet. We don't know what his agenda is. He could be an imposter, even!"

"You think it might be a scam?" She got up, pacing the room once again as she pieced the information together.

"Sure, why not? It's a good premise. He can play the sympathy card, get lots of moola, live large as a forgotten Kennedy. Pretty smart."

"Seems like a lot of trouble to prove, though. Do you think his birth certificate identifies his real parents?"

"Doubt it, not after all the effort to keep him mum. Plus there's always PhotoShop." Lee spun around in his chair.

"Such a skeptic. Typical man," Gal scoffed, tossing a wad of paper at him.

"You're a softie, typical woman," "I know someone who's not a softie," Gal purred, propping herself on the desk.

Lee's cheeks crimsoned. He thought he had concealed his weapon. *Was she up for more?* "Does that interest you?"

"Not particularly," she lied, enjoying the puzzled look on his handsome face. "Besides, you still have to call Anita and get us to Fitz."

"I will," he promised. "And then…"

"And then, you will take me on a proper date." Galaxy decided if they were going to continue their fling, she wasn't giving the goods away for free.

Chapter Eight

Covertly stepping into Galaxy's office the next morning, he nixed flipping on the light. Luckily, he convinced the janitor the night before that he left time-sensitive documents inside. Diverting Hank's attention with his favorite crab cakes from Phillips Seafood didn't hurt either. It kept him busy while Lee pressed the key into duplicating putty.

He touched the envelope to his lips. Did he really want to do this? He had a mission to complete. Dating Gal would bog him down. They were probably better off parting ways so they could get some work done. On the other hand, wouldn't it be a perfect example of keeping your enemies close? Not that he was sure she was an enemy exactly. Or could it be, he wondered, hovering over the presentation, he was actually falling in love? The rose he left probably clinched it.

About to leave, a devious thought crossed his mind. *The secret compartment!* He shook the handle to find it locked, the same being true for the two side drawers. He half-heartedly tugged the third when it slid open, to his surprise.

Flipping through tedious files, he just about gave up until alas, hidden in the end space was a black quilted case. Looking around, he unzipped it carefully. The pouch overflowed with feminine products, which was so repelling, he nearly dumped the whole works into the cubby. Then a tri-fold of square packets caught his attention. Interesting... Was she stockpiling after he failed to do so?

Detaching a single condom, he shoved it into his pants pocket for good measure then wiped grimy film off his fingers. They weren't new! So why didn't she offer one up that first night?

Hastily re-zipping the case, the metal teeth pinched the fabric. Struggling against time to unsnag it, something shiny shook free and fell on the floor. A key! Could he be that lucky?

The click-clack of heels in the hall kept time with his pounding heart. He slipped it into his pocket, closed the drawer with his foot and peeked between the window blinds. It wasn't Gal but did he dare risk it? It was now or never. Popping the lock, he pulled the drawer to find—nothing! Disappointed, he quickly patted the perimeter just in case something stuck to the side. A loose edge lifted! Peeling back the felt, he discovered a treasure trove of trinkets.

He rustled through some papers—her visa and passport, a badge—*whoa KGB, who was she really?* He slipped it inside his jacket, tit for tat. Several silver lipstick tubes (or were they bullets?) rolled around until finally, he fished out a flip phone. Flicking it open, the screen remained black. "Outta juice," he muttered, feeling around for a charger but coming up empty.

Tossing it back, the impact jostled the screen protector loose, emitting a subtle border of light. Reclaiming it, he stripped away the black-out plastic, revealing a brightly lit display of odd fonts, Soviet he was sure. Pressing his way to the contacts file, the only listing was Firebird, all other fields blank. Curiosity begged him to scroll further, but he knew he already chewed up the clock.

Reaching into his inner pocket, he pulled out a miniature transistor device. On the off chance she still used the old thing, he pried the phone apart with a scissor blade, peeled off the bug's adhesive with his teeth and nestled it inside a groove within the housing panel. The echoes of co-workers were gaining in number, so he snapped the phone back together, and wiped it clean with his kerchief. He replaced it among the contents, plinking the key back into the case as well. Backing out of the room, he made a beeline to the cafeteria for a strong cup of coffee.

Gal was only half-awake during the elevator ride to her floor, sleep-walking down the hall, just missing Lee. On a night when she should've slept well, she tossed and turned, lecturing herself for giving him such an ultimatum, ruining everything.

He didn't exactly look enthused about courting her. Maybe he wasn't used to being put on the spot, or maybe he wasn't the wine and dine type. No, that can't be. He's such a gentleman; surely he knows how to treat a lady. Odd that he didn't give an answer to her proposition, instead immediately calling Anita to arrange a meet and greet with Fitz.

Ah, it's just business to him! Feeling foolish, she jabbed her key in the door, finding it ajar. The unsettling lurch woke her as she gave the room a defensive sweep. The cleaning crew again! She would be sure to report their incompetence this time.

When her briefcase didn't lay flat on the desk, she soon saw why. "What?" Her spirits soared as she inhaled the flowery scent. She snatched the envelope, tearing it open like she won a sweepstakes. The writing indicated an invitation, written in an attempt of childlike calligraphy. She pulled out the remainder, revealing…a cocktail napkin. She shook her head, chuckling.

Please join me for an evening of champagne and dancing

at the Dandridge Hotel and Ballroom, Georgetown

Saturday @ 7pm

Gal fell backward into her chair and spun around. He *was* the dating type! Relieved now that she knew Lee was a man of action, she warned herself to play it cool. She couldn't get attached. *This is a job, not a romance.* It was becoming her mantra, but she wasn't following it very well. Still, she couldn't deny the floating sensation whenever she was with him. When she realized she was holding a napkin to her chest, she reprimanded herself for being silly. She needed to get some work done. Springing up to grab a coffee, she bumped into Lee, who arrived equipped with two steaming to-go cups.

"Oh, thanks! I was just about to go get one." She caught her breath, the proximity of his strong build causing mild arrhythmia.

"I took a chance you might be in," he smiled, extending his offering. "It's double cupped so be careful; it's hot."

"Yes, is it," she agreed, staring at his chest. Lee took the hint and kissed her, a sweet, business appropriate smooch that held the promise of passion later on.

Feeling self-conscious when their lips parted, Galaxy was grateful when her eyes fell back on her desk. "Thank you," she said, scooping up the fancy lettering. "Surely this can't be the same one from lunch. So, a night of bubbly and bopping…is that what you Americans call dancing?"

Lee chuckled, reclining leisurely on her desk. "Could be, but bopping has another meaning too." He wagged his finger between them. "It's sorta what we've been doing lately."

"Ah, so tangos and waltzes then?" she smiled, swiveling in her chair.

"Well…" His voice trailed off, and he decided to leave it at that. Resting on the desk corner, he stretched his long arm to place his coffee on an end table. "So is that a yes? Does it meet your specifications?"

"We'll see."

"We'll see, that's your answer?" he laughed in disbelief.

She smiled. "Who knows, I might have to wash my hair. We'll see how things pan out. If you're still taking notes, bowling or dinner would be fine too."

"I went for the big guns too soon, huh? You seem more like the caviar type."

"Why, because I'm Slavic?" She crossed her arms, a bit offended.

"No, because you're elegant and beautiful."

She eyed him carefully. "And… you're forgiven. But nah, I can't stand the stuff. I'm up for anything fun. I'm flexible."

"True dat," Lee mumbled.

Just then the boss popped in. "Good morning, any leads?"

They scrambled to their feet. "Morning, Geoff. We're interviewing a potential suspect today," Lee offered. Gal wasn't sure how much they should reveal, so she concentrated on her coffee.

"So you figured out who then?" Geoff's eyes brightened with interest. He took a pen out his jacket and opened his folder.

"Yes, we're on the trail of a likely culprit. It sounds a bit out there, but we think he is the illegitimate son of JFK, seeking revenge."

"What? You mean Junior left behind a legacy? The most eligible bachelor of his time?" Geoff beamed, scribbling furiously at this spicy morsel.

"No, sir, we mean Senior," piped Gal. "And well, Marilyn Monroe."

Their boss clicked his pen several times in aggravation then snapped his padded folder shut. "Don't waste your time falling for tabloid hogwash. I want a real solution, understand?" He pointed his portfolio at them, leaving as curtly as his words.

Lee closed the door and whistled.

"Now what?" Gal asked, slumping in her chair. "We give up?"

"No, we're spies, aren't we? We can do anything

under the radar. I don't want to quit now, especially after all the effort we put in making connections."

"Did you reach Anita? You were calling her when I left."

"As a matter of fact…" He reached into his jacket, flashing a business card. "I met up with her, and she gave me ol' Fitzy's number."

Gal jumped up. "You've been sitting on this and not telling me?"

"Well, we were discussing our date, and then Geoff barged in. I got his voicemail when I called, but we have an appointment in a couple of hours." Lee glanced at his watch. "We better go."

"Now? I thought…" It didn't make sense, but she grabbed her purse when Lee motioned toward the door.

"We have to pick up a little something first."

Feeling a tad nervous, she climbed into Lee's Mustang. The last time they left the office, they became embroiled in a most unusual adventure. What was he so eager to pick up along the way, prophylactics? Did he think scheduling a date was the same as having already gone on one? Fuming at the nerve of his macho ego, she couldn't help wonder where they would wind up next.

Jumping on Key Highway, they sputtered through construction delays, leaving Maryland behind and shooting past the District of Columbia on 495, at last merging on Route 1 toward Virginia.

When the ignition cut off, Galaxy was staring at a taupe Colonial with the iconic picket fence, columned porch, pretty slate shutters and an Alexandria Realtors sign staked on the lawn.

Stepping out, she was hesitant but couldn't contain her curiosity. "Fitzy lives here?"

"No, you'll see."

"It's a bit fast for us to be shacking up, isn't it?"

She was glad when he laughed, but still a little wary it could be true.

The doorbell summoned a barking dog, followed by a blonde woman slightly younger than Lee. He gave her a kiss on the cheek. A small boy pushed past, happy to see him.

Gal's heart sunk. He said he wasn't married, but she never asked if he ever had been. She eyed the child, an anxious pang tightening her chest.

Lee turned to see Gal's bewildered face and was about to explain when the boy shouted, "Unca Ree, come see the Rego Deaf Star I just builded…"

Gal exhaled in relief. The kid hung off his arm as they shuffled inside. Uncle Monkey Bars introduced Gal to his sister Lainey and nephew Travis, who didn't waste time pulling him into the open family room.

"Elaine," his sister corrected, extending her hand. "Well, technically it's Shelby Elaine, but he still calls me by my kid nickname." She rolled her eyes in his direction. "Leland, it's not like I still call you Bubba."

Gal snickered at both names, childhood banter alive and well.

"Touché, Hermit Crab."

"I was a bookworm and didn't get out much, so

the kids in town cleverly cooked *that* one up."

"I was head chef," Lee admitted with a wink, snapping Legos together.

"Well, you can call me Lainey if you want. It's so nice to meet you. Lee never brings girlfriends over."

"Likewise, but we're just co-workers," she blushed. "Did you go abroad for finishing school, too? Were you—what do they call it—a debutante?"

"Oh, yes, we had to suffer through those pesky etiquette classes, but we didn't go to finishing school." Pouring coffee, she placed a hand on her hip, addressing Lee with a laugh as he strolled into the kitchen. "Are you still trying to impress the ladies with that line?"

"Why, you phony…" Gal smacked his arm, amused.

"Hey, you were the one to guess it. I just played along."

"He did get sent away, though. That much is true. Pops shipped him off to military school one summer after he set the neighbor's barn on fire."

Gal about sprayed them with a mouthful. "You did not!"

Lee looked sheepish. "I told you I was hell on wheels."

"He and a bunch of hooligans swiped old Zebadiah's tractor, plow and tiller and the morons decided to race. I don't know what you were thinking."

"Wrong day to be bored. I bet them the tractor could outrun horsepower. We were fourteen and all hyped about cars. Horsepower sounded so fast, you know? We wanted to see for ourselves." Guffawing at the stupidity, he continued. "Well, the horses were dragged down by all that hardware so even clocking the max at 25 mph, I was whizzing right past the beasts. But Billy Bob's horse got spooked and made a sudden turn. I over-corrected to avoid him, crashing into the barn, which ignited like kindling!"

"Goodness, Lee! Did you get hurt?" Gal reached out, stroking his arm in concern, but had to admit she liked this side of him.

"He got banged up, but it was the hay bales that saved you, wasn't it?" Lainey rose to pluck a basket of just-baked muffins from the island, not missing a clue. *Coworkers, my foot!*

"Hay? That's flammable, isn't it?"

"Yes, but the tractor plowed right into a stack of the stuff, creating a makeshift tunnel, padding me before completely incinerating. Billy's quick grab of the fire extinguisher saved the day. I was fortunate to limp away with a few first degree burns, stitches and a dislocated knee. But boy, old man Zeb was pissed!"

"No doubt. He made you boys work off the damage instead of pressing charges. You're lucky he was so lenient. Plus Pops promised him he'd have you whipped into shape at the Academy."

"West Point?" Gal asked, tearing off a hunk of strudel topping.

"Marine Military Academy. And it's as strict as it sounds. Hated it at first but it wasn't all bad. There was time for outdoor fun. I ended up doing the last three years of high school there, and it *did* inspire me to go to West Point so I can't say I regretted it. Put me on the right path." Grabbing a crumbly treat, he turned it upside to eat bottom first.

Gal was impressed. "Wow, you really turned things around. Wait, you said shoving a kid into a locker got you banished."

"Oh, a caboodle of crime got me exiled. The barn was just the last *straw*."

The women groaned as he collected the cups and saucers and washed them in the sink. "So, how's the house sale going, Sis?"

"Slow, but I'm glad we have this showing this morning. It's impossible to keep the house clean with a four-year-old." Just then the sheepdog lumbered in, showing off a rawhide rope toy and plunking down with a loud thud. "And especially this guy! I'm so glad you offered to take Harold to the park today."

Gal's head was spinning from this strange detour. "We came to pick up Harold?"

"Yes, it helps them out and also gives us a little break from the *office*," he nudged. "It's so stuffy being cooped up in a cubicle."

"Oh, right. That's a great idea! It's a beautiful spring day, so a park break sounds lovely." She bent down to pet the dog, who resembled a mop. His eyes were hard to see through all the fleece.

"Thanks, Lee. Stay for lunch when you bring him back. You too, uh, Galaxy was it?"

Gal was impressed she got it right, despite Lainey's transparent tone. "Yes, my mother's dream was to become an astronaut, but in those Ukrainian times, she was discouraged. So she's a science teacher."

"Oh, it's a shame she had to give it up." Lainey clipped Harold's leash on him and handed the reins to Lee.

"Yeah, but she's happy teaching. She says rockets would've made her space sick anyway!"

Lee listened, fascinated as the girls laughed, wondering if any of it was true. It sounded credible enough, but with secret agents, you never could tell. "Well, good luck, Sis! I hope this is the bite you need to sell the house."

Out on the porch, Gal quipped, "I hope it's the only thing that bites."

"Ol' Harry here is a harmless rug," he assured, giving the dog an affectionate scratch. It took both of them to squeeze him into the car.

"Why exactly are we bringing the dog with us?" Gal asked between sloppy kisses from her new friend.

"You'll see," Lee hinted as they drove into the city.

Gal wasn't sure she was up for another surprise.

They parked, then went for a stroll. Harold was in his glory, running to each hydrant and cherry blossom tree until he spotted a squirrel. He made a mad dash for the rodent, nearly pulling Lee's arm out of the socket. Gal chased after them, heels in hand.

When she caught up at a corner, her hair had escaped the loose bun but Lee's demise was much worse—a jumbled mess with three other dog leads wrapped around his legs, tying up his ankles.

"Oh no, the dog walker!" Gal fretted, their lie the day before coming true. She tried unraveling the cords before he tripped but got wound up too. The canine chaos only made things worse as Lee and Gal faced each other tethered in knots. When they fell together, Gal on top with tumultuous waves spilling over her face, they both started laughing.

"What were you saying about Twister?" she teased.

"Hmm, nice… pink zebra!"

She looked down to see her push-up bra playing peekaboo. Lee couldn't resist and kissed her anyway. It was a good thing all the barking and traffic reminded them they were on a public street.

"Cool your biscuits, hombre," Gal ribbed, feeling the usual arousal. "So…this is why we went out of our way to pick up your sister's dog?"

"No, he is!" Lee gestured to the figure standing over them, unknotting the labyrinth of leashes.

Chapter Nine

Gal looked up and realized the dog walker she had seen yesterday wasn't female after all, although he did sport the same shock of black curly hair and lime green tourist hoodie. It was odd attire for a man in his fifties.

Once the bunch of loops loosened, they stepped out of the woven mess, thanking him for the rescue.

"I hope none of the pups were hurt," she offered, brushing off her skirt and readjusting her fuchsia top with the cloak collar.

"They seem to be fine." The nervous man with the nasal voice examined each paw. He straightened, sliding his round, wire frames up the bridge of his nose, looking more like a mad scientist than someone who exercised canines.

"This is embarrassing," Lee began. "I was bringing you a client. I heard you were the best around."

"Oh thanks, is that what you heard? These pooches are my best friends. They're all I have." His brown eyes clouded over.

"I can tell you love them," Gal said. "We feel the same about Harold." She ruffled his frayed yarn.

"I do. They're the only ones who listen to me. They never interrupt. No one else takes me seriously." He gave the canines a quick scratch behind the ears, then sensing he was disclosing too much, flipped back to professional mode. "Well, my rate is fifty an hour. I'm Fitz, by the way," he introduced himself. "From Kennedy Kennels and Dog Walking."

"Oh, I'm Lee-um-Louis, and this is… Gail," Lee stammered, sharing a knowing smile with Galaxy, who wanted to slug him.

Fitz shook their hands. "Glad to meet you, Liam Louis and Gail." He whispered their names three times. When he saw their skeptical expressions, he explained. "Oh, that's a memory trick."

"I'll have to try that sometime. Did you say Kennedy Kennels? Must be great for business in this area. Are you related to the former president?" Gal asked, not wasting time.

Fitz squirmed. "Well, I *am*, not that anyone believes me. That's the problem!" He scrunched his brows and Gal could see a fleck of anger in his pupils as he yanked a clump of hair.

"I suppose there are a lot of Kennedys out there," Lee suggested. "All trying to get a piece of the prestigious pie."

"But I bet if everyone traced their roots, it would lead to the same family tree," Gal soothed, not wanting to ignite any craziness. It was obvious Fitzy was a lit fuse.

"But I truly *am!* I'm a direct descendant of JFK. My mother was famous too, you know, but they just wanted to cover *that* up. A big hush-hush over politics and Hollywood. So not fair! They still want to snuff me out even though they're both long gone." He kicked a metal trash receptacle.

"I'm sure you are, Fitz." She patted his arm. "Wait—Fitz, is your actual name, Fitzgerald, as in your father's middle name? Has anyone done a DNA test? There must be a way to prove it."

Fitz ran his free hand through his unruly hair. "Yes, it is, not that anyone will listen to me to even try it." His left eye twitched. It was starting to spasm, and he didn't want to make a bad first impression, so he pretended to adjust his lopsided glasses. "Hey, don't worry about me. I have my business and furry friends to keep me busy. If I didn't have this, I'd die of loneliness. Did you want me to walk your dog too?" He reached for the leash.

"Well, to be truthful, we'd like to get to know you better before we entrust our dog to you," Lee stated. "Do you have a business license or something we can see?"

Fitz frowned. "Wait a minute. Are you two cops or something? What's your deal? Did those White House narcs hire you to trail me? I swear, I only tried putting pressure on them to give me my rightful heritage. It wasn't a threat as they say. I didn't mean to set the flag on fire. Honest."

"Oh my, Fitz. No, we aren't cops but how did that happen?" Gal exchanged a troubled glance with her partner. No wonder Anita seemed upset that he was on the premises.

"I got mad when they tried escorting me out the door. I had a lighter in my pocket. It calms me to flick it. I guess I went too far because it flared up instead. I'm a smoker. I know, I know, I'm trying to quit. But never mind me, it's not important. We are here for the dogs."

"Oh wow. Did your pants catch fire?" Lee meant it sincerely but couldn't help feeling amused at the double meaning.

"No, it was in my hand, thank goodness. I just happened to be close to the drapes."

"Those too?" Gal's stomach knotted. This was getting out of hand fast.

He reached again for the leash.

"We just don't know where you live or where

you'll take Harold. What's your route, you know, in case we need to pick him up early?" Lee was reluctant to hand over the dog as if he ever intended to.

"Yeah, the last walker we hired didn't run her charges. She just tied the dogs to a bicycle rack while she sipped away at the cyber cafe," Galaxy said. Lee was impressed, almost believing it until he remembered they only borrowed Harold a few minutes ago.

Fitz looked them over carefully. "So, what do you want to know? I gotta start moving. The natives are getting restless." He motioned to the two collies and Great Dane who were starting to wrestle.

"We'll walk with you. So, where's your main office?" Gal was wary of the herd ahead, not wanting to trip again.

"I work from home. All I need is a cell phone, no overhead cost. My place doesn't allow pets, so this business is the best of both worlds."

"So, there aren't any kennels? That's false

advertising," Lee probed, testing tempered waters.

"Well, no, it's just the name of the b-b-business. Like a t-title of a b-book, right?" Fitz stood his ground but showed signs of distress.

"Book titles hint at what books are about," Lee agitated. "If I was reading Leo Tolstoy's *War and Peace* and it was about a flower arranging elf, I'd be pretty damn mad."

Beads of sweat dampened his hairline. "Oh, man," he whined, pulling on his upper lip. "I never thought about it th-that way. Is it against the l-aw?"

"No, it's not, Fitz," Gal reassured, patting his arm again. "Companies do it all the time."

Lee glared, exasperated. *What was she doing?* He tried once more. "So, you spend all day with mutts, huh? It must get lonely."

"Yeah, don't you crave human interaction?" Gal added, nervously following his lead.

"Well, yeah, of course," he trembled, a shadow ebbing over him. "It just doesn't work out. People tend to write me off. They -t-tell me I g-give off a w-weird vibe." He looked like he would become unglued at any moment. Would he unveil more information about his life? Lee and Gal were on the edge of their seats. Just then, they turned a corner and Fitz adjusted the leashes. "I'm having an interaction now with you unless you're not human?"

"You got me there," Gal smiled, feigning a laugh. "But what I meant is, do you have a significant other? It's so much better to share your life with someone special." She made doe eyes at Lee.

Fitz followed her gaze, a tad irritated. "Are you newlyweds or something?"

Lee chuckled. "No, we've been married for ten years, but hey man, your private life is none of our business. Sorry if Gail was too nosy. She's like that."

Gal grabbed Lee's hand, forcing a bubbly smile. "Yeah, sorry Fitz. When I'm in love, I just want the whole world to be in love too."

"Th-Th-That's nice," he stammered. "Well, there's this lady who works at the bakery. I'm kinda sweet on her I guess. She gives me extra frosting when I order my daily cupcake." Fitz stopped and pointed to a shop across the street, The Affectionary Confectionary.

"Oh, that sounds promising," Gal squealed. "Maybe you should ask her out. I know it's nerve-racking at first, but keep it simple."

"Nah, I don't know. In case you haven't noticed, I'm not exactly a ladies' man. I wouldn't want to screw up a good thing. Look, you guys seem like nice folks, but I have to return these pups to their owners soon and pick up a few more. I haven't done their grooming yet. I always return a dog in tip top shape—that's the Kennedy way."

"Well, that's an extra benefit I'm sure their owners appreciate. You know what? I'm sure we can make a permanent arrangement to walk Harold. Right, Liam?"

"Yeah, we'll talk it over. Nice meeting you, Fitz." Lee extended his hand, leaving him near the diner.

"Wait just a second," Fitz called, trotting after

them, his Iditarod crew leading the way.

Lee and Gal flinched before turning around. Had he caught onto them?

He dug into his pocket, producing lint and a business card. "If you decide, give me a call. I'm out of town next week so think fast."

On the drive back to Alexandria, Harold crammed his head out the window, drooling all over Gal's neck. "Did I mention I'm not much of a dog person?" she asked, reaching for a tissue.

Lee grinned. "I'll add it to the list. So what did you think of Fitz?"

"He sure likes to bank on the Kennedy name."

"Probably good for business but I'm not buying it. I don't see any resemblance to either alleged parent. Do you think he's harmless?" They went into a tunnel, and Harold ducked back in.

"I'm not sure. He seems a bit unstable. I was getting nervous when he started to lose it," Gal confessed. "Even though we were the ones prodding him."

"Yeah, I was trying to get him to reveal his plan. He was on the verge, but you kept calming him down."

"Sorry, I didn't know what he'd do or if he had a gun."

"*We* have guns," Lee reminded. "It's fine if he goes off the deep end. In fact, our job depends on him doing just that."

"When he started to rave about the White House, he must've realized he was giving too much away. Even so, a lost Kennedy hardly seems dangerous. There must be something deeper going on."

"Hey, I remember reading about a possible mafia triangle between Sinatra's Rat Pack and the Kennedys. Maybe Fitz is a mob boss."

The ridiculous theory caused a convulsion. Fitz could barely manage pooches.

"Guess we'll have to trail him to find out. Why do you think he's out of town next week? Do you think he's giving up?" Lee continued.

"I got the opposite feeling like maybe he's planning something drastic. I wish we could follow him now. Too bad we have to go back to your sister's. How come she lives around here if you're both from Texas?"

"Her husband's a senator, but his term ended. They're moving back to Galvo when their house sells. He resumed his law practice, so he travels back and forth."

"Oh, well it's nice that you have family close. Mine are all in Ireland with a few scattered in the Soviet Union." Gal reached behind her head to pat Harold.

"So, it's true?"

"Yes, of course, it's true. I wouldn't lie to you." She was confused and a little insulted. "I didn't mean to tell you my family background earlier. I hope you aren't scared off by the Russian stereotype—people usually are—but really, it's more Crimean and mostly Irish."

"Yeah, I have to say it did startle me a bit. But

it's not like you're an assassin or anything, right?" He chuckled uneasily, her odd desk gadgets coming to mind.

"Absurd," she tittered. "I come from very good people. My father is a dentist. Well, oral surgeon, really. He works with Doctors Without Borders."

"Charitable. Saving the world one wisdom tooth at a time?"

Gal beamed. "Usually, but right now he's part of Smile Train, fixing cleft lips on children in India."

"Wow, very selfless, although a dentist still sounds a bit torturous. But I was asking if it was true how you got your name."

"Yes, remarkably, it is. My mom teaches astronomy at the University of Dublin. She escaped the area at nineteen, somehow finding her way on a boat to Ireland where she met my dad. He helped her get into college. A chance came up for her to get into a space program but by then she was pregnant with me, so abracadabra, there you have it."

"So, does that mean you have a sister named

Milky Way or a brother named Worm Hole?" Lee joked, kissing her hand.

Gal burst into a fit of giggles. "Close, I have a brother named Orion. And our cat is named Milky Way."

"No way! Or are you pulling *my* cord now?"

"Perhaps, *Bubba*."

Lee cringed, nodding amicably. "Okay, funny. Lainey couldn't say brother, and the name stuck."

"That's so cute," Gal purred. "But you know, if you want, I can pull something else, Cowboy." She let her fingers do the walking on his pant leg.

"Hmm. I'd take you up on it if ol' Harry here weren't panting down my shirt."

"What dog? That's me." They exchanged a playful smile.

"That was some tie-up earlier, huh?" he sighed, reminiscing. "I almost wasn't able to get up right away."

"Yeah, I know. With you, that's always a problem." She gave his thigh a squeeze.

"Just thinking of you falling on top of me, looking so tousled. Damn sexy!" he whistled. "If we weren't expected at my sister's any minute now..."

"So....let's be late," she whispered, massaging his earlobe, this time making the hair on *his* neck stand.

"What about him?" Lee asked, distracted.

"Clip him to a tree," she suggested. "Or I can take care of things on the way. Your choice." She unzipped his fly.

Her offer blew his mind. He swerved, the thrill of it almost making him take the chance, but he preferred to enjoy it freely, not kill anyone in the process. He switched lanes and speed off the next exit. "There's an abandoned base down the road," he explained. "We used to have practice there until they demolished the place."

Rolling past several "No Trespassing" signs, the tires crunched on gravel as they entered the grounds hosting several dilapidated barracks. Some were burned to the ground exposing their foundations, others in an array of ruin. A few windows, either burnt out or broken, were protected by graffiti-plastered planks.

The blackened shells triggered a suffocating memory. *Swelling smoke, an enemy bullet hitting her machine gun's gas chamber igniting the blast. Viktor almost didn't get to her in time. If he hadn't...* She shivered, remembering to breathe.

"You alright?" Lee rested his hand on her arm.

"Yeah, fire creeps me out. I'm glad we're here in the daytime. Was this military school?"

"Nope, that was in Harlingen, practically Mexico. This place was just softball during training academy. It used to be a Navy Annex."

"I hope it wasn't this crispy when you played here."

"No, they closed the base years ago. Then it became the fire department's training camp." Lee parked as far back as he could, winding up behind the old Commissary store. They would be somewhat hidden in the jungle of overgrown grass, away from the devastation.

"Hang on, okay?" He jumped out and hooked Harold's leash to the metal railing, lengthening it all the way so the pooch could roam, then dashed back to escort Gal to their latest quest.

They looked for a secluded place among the wildflowers, the vibrant splash of colors a contrast against the charred remnants and stale sting of cinder. As they settled on the ground, Gal wondered about pollen-stained suits.

"Ah, there's a blanket in the trunk with the safety gear." He hurried to the vehicle and came back with the solution. "It's not much, but it's better than nothing."

"Tin foil?" Gal giggled at first glance.

They laid back on the crinkly silver, watching the puffy clouds for a minute. "It's like a space suit or something." Gal fingered the thin, metallic material. "Would this even keep someone warm?"

"I think it stems from NASA technology, so you should feel right at home on it."

"Ha, very funny!" She sat up and began unbuttoning her blouse, but his impatience pulled her on top, rewarding him with his favorite eyeful. Slanting forward, her burgundy streaks tickled his nose.

Lee played with her hair, twirling it up and to the side, then brought her face close for a tender kiss. "Hey, I've restocked," he whispered, proudly producing the packet he swiped earlier. Clamping it between his teeth, he started to tear it open.

"Stop!" Gal warned, alarmed. "Where did you find that?"

Ut-oh. He sat up, busted. "Well, I, uh, saw them in your bottom drawer. Apparently, you do keep a Boy Scout kit. Why didn't we break into your stash the other night?"

"Because they're poisonous! Didn't you read the label?"

Lee's vision zoomed in. **Condemns**. "Why do you have these?" Distressed, he ditched the pouch, looking wildly for a place to wash his hands.

"I told you I had an arsenal." She sprinted to the car and grabbed antibacterial wipes from her purse.

Lee sat there stunned, his face turning a humiliating hue. "I'm beginning to believe you. Should I swig a bottle of Ipecac?"

"You barely dented the foil. You'll be fine," she laughed. "That will teach you to snoop. What exactly were you looking for?"

"Just wanted to see if you started a case file on Fitz. Are you sure I'll be okay?"

"If I was worried, would I do this?" she purred, frenching him deep. "Besides, I would never use them on you, only my wicked enemies."

"You sleep with your enemies?" he sputtered.

"I never said *that*," she glibbed, tugging at his belt. "And I've already taken care of things for us." She flashed a safer version from her pocket.

Sighing relief, he thrust off his pants, pushing Gal back on the blanket for a frisky session. Afterward, bathed in the warmth of sun and endorphins, they slowly pieced themselves back together, astonished that the best they ever had—so far—was in a daisy field, no less. Their laughter and Harold's barking nearly drowned out the buzzing of his phone.

"This is getting ridiculous, Tom! Now Fitz is demanding his mother get full recognition at the Mother's Day Tea on Friday? He's nuts. It's not even fitting. It's to honor military moms and first ladies, not Hollywood harlots and White House homewreckers."

"So, what, who cares? He's harmless. Blow him off."

"Yeah, right, so he can blow us up instead? You call that harmless?"

"Probably just one of his empty threats."

"We can't take that chance, can we? He says he's planted a bomb somewhere on the premises. So now we either give Monroe her due or cancel the whole event. Neither is fair."

"Let's sweep the place. Call SWAT. Confirm his bluff."

"And let the media catch wind of it? Exposure is exactly what he wants."

"I'll alert the service; we'll keep this six feet deep. We can send in EOD specialists disguised as caterers or something."

"Hey, that might just work," Anita brightened as they scuffled out of the room.

"Cripes, he's taken it to the next level," Gal fretted, fastening buttons in a flash.

"We better go round him up." He scrambled to his feet, buckling up. "Maybe we can prevent a disaster."

"What about fluffy over there?"

"Dammit, we'll have to drive fast." Snatching the blanket, they quickly packed the car, helping Hal's furry behind into the back seat. Gal's leg caught the sharp edge of the door frame.

"These blasted things." She peeled off her broken nylons, bunching them up in her purse. "I'm always snagging them on file cabinets and such. You're lucky you don't have to wear them."

"Oh, I but have," he joked, kissing her nose. "Now that I think of it, I was in drag once or twice and did pop a seam." He shifted into drive, taking off.

"I hope it was for a case. And let me guess how you ripped it," she snorted, pointing to his crotch.

"Not exactly. I was escaping a scene and had to jump a fence. Split the whole works in two! I had to get away, or I was going to end up in a shotgun wedding."

Gal laughed so hard her side hurt. "Sounds like a good movie."

"It was, almost. Speaking of which, I owe you one."

"We have champagne and dancing."

"Yes, but if we're keeping score, I'm racking up quite a tab. Hey, there's an old film fest at the park tonight! Believe it or not, they're playing Billy Wilder's *Some Like It Hot*."

"Oh, sounds fun. What's it about?"

"Appropriate in two ways. Jack Lemmon and Tony Curtis dress as women and sneak on an all-girl train. I forget why."

"Ooh, funny. I hope they have better luck with pantyhose. What's the second reason?"

"The leading lady is Marilyn Monroe."

Chapter Ten

Snarled in construction back up on 395 North, Lee jumped ship and snaked his way to Route 1, cutting through the National Air and Space Museum into downtown D.C.

"It'll only get worse this summer," he complained. "What are the odds we find Fitz?"

"Pretty good, I'd say. Do you think Lainey was suspicious? She was acting weird."

Lee looked over. "Maybe it's the dandelion stems," he laughed, plucking a few from the back of her head.

"Why didn't you say anything?" Gal's cheeks flared as she dug a compact from her purse, weeding the rest.

"I just noticed. My clothes are all wrinkled. She probably put two and two together, but she's cool."

As they waited at a light near the bakery, Gal

spotted the culprit. "Hey, look who it is, with a skip in his step. I wonder if he asked her out yet. Is it odd that he doesn't have any dogs?"

"He must be between clients. Or maybe I should say Claw-ents."

Gal shook her head. "Let's follow him. Maybe we'll see where he lives."

They crept slowly behind, annoying other drivers. All the honking made Fitzy paranoid. He started flipping people off randomly, muttering obscenities along the way, only increasing gridlock and blaring horns.

A cement mixer swerved in front, cutting them off. The driver hopped down from his cab, ready to give the raving lunatic a piece of his mind.

The agents exchanged worried looks. "Oh no, Lee, should we intervene?"

"Let's sit tight and see how it plays out. Maybe we'll catch an incriminating rant. With front row seats, all we need now is popcorn."

"You're awful," Gal chuckled as they watched

the scene roll.

"Hey, Mack," the angry Teamster sputtered in Fitz's face. "What's your problem? You're causing road rage. You better simmer down." He extinguished his cigarette deep into the lofty frosting.

Gal gasped, hand over mouth.

"Hey! Not cool," he wailed. "You owe me a cupcake."

"You better keep your gestures and mouth to yourself, freak. Don't think I don't see you around on the street corners begging for money, walking mutts. You probably don't clean up after them either." The meaty man menaced, dwarfing Fitz, who in his defense, produced a roll of baggies from his pocket.

A punch in the mouth or a bone-breaking pummeling wouldn't do them any good, so Lee popped the handle and jogged over, Gal close behind.

"Hey buddy, that's enough. He's just a harmless dog walker. "

"Stay out of it, pal. What are you, his psych

warden?"

"Parole officer." Lee flashed his badge too quick to read. "Do you need one too?"

"Come here, we'll get you a new treat." Gal lured Fitz to neutral territory, and he strolled over, baffled. To the driver, she explained. "Sorry he caused you trouble. He's a little off. Gets triggered by loud noises is all."

They ushered him toward the car, the trucker still flapping his yap. Once inside the safety of the vehicle, Fitz came out of his daze, recognizing them. "Hey, it's you guys from earlier today. How did you know I hate loud noises?"

"Just a guess. My grandma's like that," Gal sympathized, gaining trust.

"Where can we drop you?" Lee asked, trailing the mixer as it maneuvered on.

"It's my afternoon break," he began, brooding over his nicotined topping.

"First stop, bakery. Hey, a good excuse to see your sweetie again," Gal sang, handing Fitzy a five as

Lee circled the block.

When he sauntered out with a replacement and two coffees, they strolled across the street and hung out on a park bench.

"So, what's your next move?" Lee asked, cutting to the chase.

"Um, with Sarah?" he asked, licking a circumference of icing.

"No, the White House. What are you going to do to get to the bottom of your name?"

"Yes, it's not right how they booted you out," Gal agreed between sips.

"Oh, well, I have some ideas." With blue frosting smeared around his lips, it was hard to believe he could do anything treacherous.

"Such as…" Lee probed.

"Wow, you guys want to hear what I have to say? I'm usually cut off mid-sentence." He eyed their interest. "I thought you just wanted me to walk your dog. Are you really a parole officer? I don't have any priors."

"We're public defenders," Lee lied. "It's our job to bring justice. But if you don't want our help, we'll move along. We have other clients to meet." They rose, playing the bluff, tossing their cups into a bin.

"W-wait. I don't know you that w-well. How do I know you can be trusted?" Fitz followed them, not willing to throw away friends.

"That's a chance you'll have to take," Gal dangled, matter-of-fact.

"Okay, what can I do legally? Sue? I was gonna break into the Oval Office and look for documents."

"I don't think they keep records there." Lee struggled to keep a straight face. "But we can arrange a DNA test. Why don't you come with us now? I know a clinic."

"I d-don't have time. I, uh, have a d-dog in ten minutes." He fiddled with a hoodie string, his eye twitching again. "And w-what about your other cl-clients?"

"We don't have an appointment for an hour," Lee informed, checking his watch. "We can squeeze you in. Are you sure you have a dog to walk? It doesn't seem like you do."

"I d-do so, two in fact. A p-poodle and a p-pit bull mix. How about we reschedule for t-tomorrow?"

"The clinic is just a block away, and we're authorized to cut the line. There's no time like the present so let's bank on it. Come on." Gal tugged his sleeve.

"No, I can't. I t-told you…leave me alone!" He pried her fingers free, dropping the cupcake in the process, then backed away, clearly distressed. Looking bewildered, he scanned the street before reaching under his sweatshirt to unzip his fanny pack.

Gal dove into defense mode, slipping off a shoe and grasping the spike of her heel while Lee positioned his hand on the pistol inside his blazer. The trick was to act swiftly without giving themselves away.

The sun reflected off a metal object in Fitz's hand as he brought it up and center. Lee aimed at his shoulder, lunging to shield Galaxy just as she scythed the stiletto at Fitzy, stabbing Lee's right triceps instead.

Baker watched in confusion, puffing on an inhaler. "You're FBI. I knew it!" He bolted off in a panic.

"No, we really aren't! I promise you." Her voice trailed after him, and she started to jog his way but her attention shifted to Lee.

"I'm good," he assured. "Go get him!"

"I can't. We need to get you to the hospital."

"For a heel scratch? Malarkey." He brushed himself off, then feeling woozy, stumbled over to a fire hydrant, taking a seat.

"They're poison darts."

His eyes bulged in panic.

"Wait, I have an antidote in here somewhere." She fumbled through her purse, pulling out a wrapped mint and a pen injector.

"Candy?" he shrieked. "How does that help?"

She shoved the dissolving tablet into his mouth,

then peeled off his jacket sleeve to stab the muscle.

After a few minutes, Lee stood, feeling stronger, until a wave of nausea knocked him off his feet. He staggered to the curb to rid himself of the toxin.

Galaxy wiped his perspiring brow, helping him to the car. "Maybe I should drive."

He jingled the keys in agreement.

Once inside, they exhaled against the headrests. Gal pounded the steering wheel in frustration. "I can't believe we blew it. Fitz is long gone by now."

"Yeah, he'll never trust us again. But what the hell, Galaxy? You run around in poison pumps? Should I go to the hospital? I can't move my arm."

"I'm sorry. You'll be fine; it's just a little botulism. I think."

"You Botoxed me? You're not sure?"

"Not intentionally." She looked down at her feet. "Yes, it's the *right* one. Whew, you'll live. Don't worry, it's just a wee more than a micro-dose."

"*More*, that's supposed to comfort me? And how can you be so sure? It's in the heel of a shoe!"

"Relax, I'm a nurse. I can dose in my sleep. The tweed probably absorbed most of it, plus the serum and Ipecac tablet kicked in." She caressed his arm softly, kissing his cheek. "Thanks for taking a bullet for me. You have my back, and that means a lot."

"Well, you certainly got mine," he winced, shrugging off the jacket's remainder. "Will it need Neosporin or something?"

"Don't be a baby," she teased. "It's just a needle."

Chapter Eleven

A canvas of pink brushstrokes streaked the sky, greeting Lee and Gal as they entered the park. The Green was filling up fast, dotted with blankets. An inflatable movie screen was tied securely between two trees.

"Let's grab that spot." With his good arm, Lee gestured to an area off to the side, away from the crowd.

"But we won't be able to see," she protested. When he arched his eyebrows, she lightly poked his chest. "We're here on a respectable date, remember? You promised. Besides, after all the encounters we've had, you couldn't possibly have any fluid left."

"I recover fast. Honestly, it's a continuous factory. But you're right. We will behave and enjoy the flick. I'm quite exhausted, really." He haphazardly spread a cover on the grass. "I might just doze off."

Gal set the basket down and helped him straighten it. "I knew we should've rescheduled. Are you sure you're up for this?" Then she yawned, settling in. "See? I might nod off too."

"I'm fine. This will be fun and take my mind off the weird paralysis."

"Great, no hard feelings?" She took out a bottle of white wine.

"Of course not. Is that a peace offering?"

"It's a complement," she flirted, revealing a gourmet-dipped dessert box. "For the strawberries."

"You sure know how to doll up a picnic. What else you got in there?" He peeked inside the wicker bin.

"Yeah, you're feeling better alright," she chuckled in relief. "Just some light snacks. Hummus, pita chips, carrots, and celery."

"Nice." He arranged the goodies on the blanket while Gal splashed drinks into purple Solo cups.

"To a real relationship," she announced as they

clunked cheers.

"Uh, relationship?" He pretended to loosen an imaginary tie on his tee.

"What? You horn dog," she razzed, pushing on his chest. "We can't stay out of each other's pants! What else would you call it?"

"A good time," he leered, leaning in, nuzzling her ear. "A really awesome, good time..."

"You give me goosebumps when you do that," Gal murmured, the Chardonnay spilling secrets. "It drives me crazy, and then I can't resist your charms."

"I know…"

"Sneaky, Cowboy, how did you pick up on that?" She narrowed her eyes, sipping more wine.

"I'm an intuitive guy," he smiled, looking down, swirling his vino. "You look nice tonight. I like the casual clothes and your hair is different." He strummed the ends of her side ponytail.

"Well, heels and skirts don't exactly cry 'movie in the park.' You're dressed down too. I like your Henley." Her fingers followed the three button trail, admiring the unfastened top loop. "Faded turquoise brings out your eyes."

"Yeah? Thanks," he grinned, looking down at his shirt. "This old thi—" he began, then stopped, studying her face, that familiar feeling crashing back again.

"What is it? Do I have strings in my teeth?" She tossed the celery stick, self-consciously covering her mouth.

"No, you're fine. I just had the weirdest sense we've done this before."

"Ah, déjà vu?"

He shook his head to clear it. "Yeah, I must be more tired than I thought. We've had a few long days, haven't we? No complaints, it's been a real blast. And for the record, I'm relieved you ditched those dangerous daggers." He leaned back and surveyed her outfit. "You know, you look a bit nautical with the blue and white striped top, and that navy scarf thing."

"Nautical or naughty?" she teased, zig-zagging

a chip through the dip.

"Both. But I thought you wanted to behave." He could feel the chemistry percolating, and he knew they couldn't act on it here. He plunged a carrot into the creamy chickpeas then spotted someone. "Gal, look!" he whispered. "Under that tree. Is that who we think it is?"

The sun was disappearing, but a few street lamps helped Gal make out the shape hunting for a spot. "Is that Fitz?" she gasped. "Oh, of course, a Marilyn Monroe movie!" She thumped her head. "Wait a minute...you were expecting him, weren't you?"

"Not exactly, just figured the odds were high that he might show up." Lee scooped extra hummus, bigger than the cracker. "Since he fled on us, it's the perfect opportunity to keep an eye on him."

"In the dark? So, this is work, not a date." She folded her arms in disbelief.

"No, we *are* going out. It's just two birds, ya know?"

"Two birds? What does that mean? Are you two-timing me?"

"No." Lee put his hand on her shoulder, stifling a chuckle. "You've never heard the expression? Killing two birds with one stone. It's terrible now that I hear it, but it means being efficient. We don't have much time to go out and have fun and this way we get ahead in our investigation."

"Oh," she said, relieved, chewing thoughtfully on a carrot. "Yeah, that's smart, especially since Geoffrey doesn't want us sniffing down this road in the first place. Should we invite him over?"

"Well, Geoffrey might spoil the mood."

"Fitz, you goofball!" She slugged his arm, making him miss his mouth. She smothered a laugh.

"Yes, why not? We might be able to get more information. Go on," he urged, grabbing a red-checkered linen from the basket and another scoop of dip.

"Me? Why don't you?"

"Well," he muffled with his mouth full. "For

one, you just pied me with a cracker, and two, I think he trusts you more."

"Sure, you just want to stuff your face," she laughed, getting up. "Save me some." She sprinted over to where Fitz was settling in.

"Hi, Mr. Baker, uh, Kennedy. Do you remember me?" She knelt beside him on the grass, thankful for jeans and sneakers.

"Oh… hi." He half-stood, ready to split. "G-G-Gail Louis, right? Are you going to arrest me?"

"No, you can relax. We aren't cops or FBI. I'm a social worker. Liam's the public defender. Are you here alone?"

"Well, sort of…someone might be meeting me." He sat back down, rifling nervously through his popcorn.

"Oh, is it that lady friend of yours?"

"Well, yeah. Sarah, from the bakery. I want to introduce her to my mother."

"Oh, is your mom here too?" Gal asked, looking around.

"Yes, well, at least she will be." He nodded at the screen.

"Ah, yes…" She fought a panicky urge to hightail it back to Lee. "I thought maybe you meant your adoptive mom, Mrs. Baker."

"No, she lives states away. But her name isn't Baker. It's Cooper. Franny Cooper."

"Oh! Does she know you're trying to get credit for your rightful lineage? It won't hurt her feelings, will it?"

"It was her idea. She made it sound like a piece of cake so I moved here, thinking I'd walk right into the White House and be a Kennedy. Instead, they laughed me right down Pennsylvania Avenue, and I'm walking dogs for a living." He sounded forlorn as if she let him down. "But I do love dogs…"

"Oh, wow," Gal mumbled under her breath. *He truly is a little bonkers.* "I'm not sure the President's headquarters is the place to start. Do you have a birth certificate?"

"Yes, but I'm a secret, so it's very not accurate."

"Right. But it says Marilyn or Norma Jean Baker?"

"Yes! It *does* say Norma Jean. I can go get it if you'd like." He started to rise.

"No, not now, we don't want to miss the movie. Maybe tomorrow. Let me do some research and help you set this straight." Just then the lights flashed three times. "Well, I better go sit down. Liam is over there. Want to join us?"

"No, that's okay. Sarah won't be able to find me if I'm lost in the park."

"Good point. We will see you tomorrow then."

Making her way back to Lee, she had trouble stepping over the maze of people in the shadows. Her foot broke through a lemon tart, starting a slippery chain reaction. The slimy filling slid her into the next picnic couple, tripping over them and sending their bucket of fried chicken flying. Poultry parts punched other picnickers, which either provided them with an extra snack or resulted in spilled drinks and popcorn. The catastrophe seemed to end when her face landed in a bowl of mashed potatoes. Gal crawled around the blankets, apologizing profusely. She was about to reach safe territory when her elbow landed in someone's nachos.

Lee flinched, witnessing the chaos unfold and galloped to Gal's rescue, armed with a gleaming, white hanky. "Do you want fries with that, ma'am?"

She looked up, mortified. A small crowd had gathered. Were they concerned about her or mad because she spoiled their supper?

"She's okay," Lee assured a security guard who had run over. To the others, he offered to replace their food. They thanked him but assured it was unnecessary.

"That's what happens when it's dark," the KFC couple said. "I saw someone snowboard a pizza once."

"Yeah, it's not the first time," the nacho guy admitted. The crowd dispersed, and everyone settled into their space.

Lee steadied her by the elbow and led the way to their area, wiping off the buffet.

"I'm a blundering idiot."

"But you taste delicious," he declared, kissing her mashed potato nose.

"Thanks, but I feel like a world class imbecile." She pulled a wad of wet towelettes from her purse and blotted her face. She wanted to cry, but that wouldn't be professional, would it?

"Hey, no worries. I've had my share of klutz moves. Pretty hilarious at my height, right? You witnessed that this morning." He lured a sad laugh. "The good thing is, it's dark. The movie's playing, so you're out of the limelight." He studied her face, slightly illuminated by the movie projector. Even globbed with starch and soda splattered hair, she managed to look cute.

"I feel all sticky. Attractive huh? So much for impressing you, unless glow-in-the-dark cheese turns you on."

Lee hid his smile, grateful for the night sky. So

she *was* digging him after all. "Didn't you know, girls covered in fast food is my wildest fantasy? Mmm…" He started nibbling the crook of her arm, kissing his way down her legs. "But I think my favorite is lemon meringue socks!"

"I'm making out with Cookie Monster," she giggled. A few "shhh's" rose from the crowd, so she corked his mouth with a strawberry. "The movie," she whispered.

Musicians Jerry (Jack Lemmon) and Joe (Tony Curtis) are in a Chicago garage when mobsters make a hit, so they duck down and try to sneak out carrying clumsy instrument cases. But the gangster boss spots them and instructs his posse to go after the potential witnesses. Whilst on the lamb, they spot a poster advertising an all-girl jazz band, and Joe gets an idea!

Next scene, they wait nervously in line, dressed in drag, to board a train to Miami. Jerry (Daphne) doubts they can pull it off because they still look too manly and is sure they won't get by the strict headmistress. But Joe (Josephine) reminds him it's life or death, so they charm their way on and prove themselves during a jam session before hiding safely in sleeping berths. Except, their masculinity isn't exactly safe when they meet Sugar Kane, a blonde bombshell that secretes all kinds of sexy.

"Ah, there she is!" Lee whispered in Gal's ear at the sight of Marilyn. The familiar rise of goosebumps prickled her skin. She cradled herself on his left, leaning against his solid frame, her head resting on his shoulder. Was it the toll of the day or the wine? She felt safe with him, as it should be with a fellow agent. But were they working on the same side? Gal stole a glance at his striking profile enjoying the movie and wished they were.

Sugar immediately piques Jerry's interest and later he lures her to his bunk for a secret slumber party. They camp out, have "girl talk" and drinks from the flask "Daphne" claimed earlier to cover for Sugar when it tumbled from her dress during rehearsal. Jerry is delighted, but his plan goes to hell when Sugar slips out to get more booze and word gets out. Soon there's a very crowded bash in his bed! The commotion wakes Joe and he ushers everyone back to their berths before the band leaders find out.

"That's my other fantasy," Lee broke in, his voice low and deep.

Galaxy was lost in thought for a moment and didn't know what he was talking about. "Uh, what?"

"A party in my bed," he whispered. "But that's a joke unless it's just the two of us." He squeezed her shoulder reassuringly.

"True, we haven't done it there yet," she prodded with a cheesy elbow.

"Ow, I see your mishap hasn't weakened it any." Lee rubbed a rib while Gal secretly smiled. They returned their attention to the film. It was a beach scene in front of a Miami hotel.

Joe figures out a better way to get close to Sugar than Jerry's idea of having "Daphne" be her confidant. With his method, he can stay out of pantyhose with a real possibility of getting into hers. Pretending to be Junior, an oil company tycoon with a yacht and a funny "rich" accent, ups his odds of scoring compared to Daphne, who's only perks are a peek at unmentionables and a pillow fight. Meanwhile, Daphne has to fight off an actual millionaire with a yacht, mama's boy Osgood Fielding III, who doesn't take no for an answer.

Even though Joe pulls off the scam—he has Daphne distract Osgood so he could pretend to own his boat—it gets him into quite a pickle when he has to resume his role as jazz musician Josephine and be in two places at once.

The mobsters eventually realize Jerry and Joe are part of the band and catch up to them in South Beach while in town for a gangster convention…

"Wow, pretty funny," Gal said, stretching with the scrolling credits. "But I nodded off and missed the ending."

"Me, too!" Lee lamented. "And so did my butt." Groggy, they sat while everyone else gathered belongings, milling their way out of the park.

Gal stole a glance as she restocked the basket. "Ah, and what an asal," she wisecracked dreamily.

Lee turned around, mock-offended. "What did you call me? And after I gave you this fantastic date?"

"No, no," she laughed. "It's a good thing, really!"

Lee shook his head, pretending not to be convinced. "I don't know, didn't sound very nice."

"On my honor, I swear. It's Irish." They were in a catcher's position, putting things away but Galaxy was laughing so hard trying to defend her language, she tipped over backward, clutching Lee's shirt to steady herself, only to pull him on top of her.

"Oh, hi..."

"Why, hello..."

"That was an accident," she disclaimed.

"I'm glad." They kissed, enjoying the delicious intimacy. He reveled in this powerful position, a hierarchy created by cavemen, not in a domineering hair-dragging sense but the thrill-of-the-hunt, triumphant prize sort-of-way. The electricity of their pulses driven by Gal's passion and the urgent, meaningful way she kissed told him she liked it too.

With the park nearly empty, the scraping of

industrial dustpans signaled the swarm of clean-up crews. He kissed her nose and then tapped her shoulder. "C'mon," he beckoned, climbing off and standing with outreached hand.

"Forever the gentleman," she admired, taking it. She scooped up the bin while he grabbed the throw. Emerging from the wrought iron gate, Gal stooped under a street light to scratch her ankle and noticed her yellow-smudged sock was stiffened by meringue.

"Oh no, I didn't smear any food on you, did I?" The dried egg-white foam was quite itchy.

Lee examined his shirt. "Nope, I'm good. Hey, do you want to stop at my place? It's close by, and I have stain stick."

She burst out laughing. "That's the lamest pickup line ever!"

"What?" Lee defended. "It's true." When Gal gave him a skeptical look, he added, "Okay, I'm tired and don't want to drive you all the way home. But I do have Spray-n-Wash!"

"Humph, men," she joked. "I told you there was

no need to pick me up, but you insisted, to make it a real date. But you're injured, and I owe you one. And I'm beat too." *Plus it'll give me a chance to search your apartment.*

"Thanks, it's been a long day. So what did you think of the movie?"

"I like how Marilyn was a sex symbol, but she wasn't a stick figure." She scratched furiously at her stained sleeve.

"Yeah, it was a healthier body image back then," Lee said, tossing their picnic paraphernalia into the trunk. "What's up, do you have fleas?"

"Sensitive skin, I guess. So, do you find her attractive?" She tried to sound casual as she slid into the seat. It would be a relief if men today didn't expect women to look like supermodels.

"Sure, there's more to women than just their looks. What makes a woman a real sexpot is body confidence."

"Really? Where were you last year when I was a chunk?"

"I doubt that made you less beautiful," he conveyed, looking deep into her eyes. "I mean that you know. It's not bull. Oh, I remember reading yesterday that Marilyn was pregnant during the filming, so she was a little poofier than usual."

"Pregnant?" Gal asked, antsy in her seat. "You mean with Fitz? Oh wow, talk about coming full circle!"

"No, calm down," he laughed. "With Arthur Miller's baby. Her husband, the playwright. Besides, it didn't take, and it was 1958, a few years before she got involved with Jack Kennedy." Lee zoomed down the maze of streets. "Hey, do you think Fitz knew she was prego and thought the same thing you did? Maybe that's why he was there."

The uncanny conversation came screeching back. "I forgot to tell you!" Galaxy rushed, so excited she was tripping over words. "He was there because he wanted to introduce Sarah, the bakery chick, to his mother and he didn't mean his adoptive mom like I thought!"

"Wow, Norman Bates much?"

"Who?" Galaxy looked up, clueless.

"You're kidding, right? A character in Alfred Hitchcock's thriller, *Psycho*. He was deranged, owned The Bates Hotel, kept his dead mother's corpse dressed in a chair. In his mind, she still controlled him."

"Eeww, that's dreadful. Fitz really might be dangerous." She reached behind her back to brush the creepy-crawlies scurrying up her spine.

"Nah, probably not, but we should keep an eye on him just in case. Are you okay?"

Flinging off the navy blue scarf, Gal hopped about in her seat, slapping at her skin. "Dammit. Ants!"

"Guess we weren't the only ones dining al fresco." He veered over, parking on a curb. She fled, flapping fabric, flinging the freeloaders. He followed, frisking her outfit to help rid the pests.

"Never a dull moment." She snickered a self-deprecating snort as they staggered back into their seats, howling at the hilarity.

"Who needs cinema? We're the comedic duo. Oh hey, speak of the devil. Look what's playing next week." He pointed to a bus stop marquee. "When *Psycho* came out, people were afraid to take showers, can you imagine? You know, because of the famous scene with the high pitched stabbing music?"

Her face remained blank and her nose scrunched in bewilderment. That expression again. A repetitive blip sent him back in time. It was the same strange sensation that tripped his instincts a few nights ago and again earlier this evening. When she craned her head to glance at the poster, a lamp post highlighted her posterior neckline, and finally, everything made sense.

"Gal, we've met someplace before!"

Chapter Twelve

Cutting the motor behind a dark, deserted warehouse, Lee stared at the steering wheel, digesting this latest revelation.

His words had ricocheted down the empty alley, spreading an eerie sensation over Gal. Was he hallucinating, slowly dying? Was it possible she injected him with the wrong chemical?

"What are you saying?" she asked, cautiously. "We met in another life? You must be delirious! It's a side effect of the toxin. We better get you to the hospital!" She leaped out to switch places.

"It's not the poison—it's you!" He lifted his arm a little to prove it. "I keep having these warped out moments. It can't just be sleep deprivation. The first one happened the night in your office before we even begun. Gotta be a fluke, right? Fate or something. I remember clearly now."

"What do you mean?" she asked, returning to her seat. "You're scaring me."

"I'm pretty sure we had a meet-cute at a deli a few months ago. Do you remember bumping into me at the IGA?"

"Hmm, no. And believe me, I'd definitely remember you."

"Really? We reached for the ticket at the same time. You don't remember that?"

"Wait, IGA? I might have gone there once for artichokes or something when I first moved here but found it too pricey. Or maybe that was Metro Market. Regardless, both are too far from my place now."

"Yes," he whooped. "That's right! You just moved here. That girl had your magenta hair color and said she was from Europe. I remember feeling a shock when our hands touched. Is that destiny or what?"

"Or static electricity," she chortled. "As romantic as that sounds, it wasn't me. Sorry. I have burgundy streaks... see?" *Crap, even when I looked like a sweaty gym troll, he remembers!* She was on the treadmill when she got the call, deciding it was as good a disguise as any. She was sure the Coke-bottle glasses she grabbed from lost and found did the trick, even if they made her nauseous.

"Of course it's you. I know because of that memorable scar. It alarmed me, but it makes sense now, you're an agent. It's a bullet, isn't it?" Why was she playing dumb? He was sure this was more than just a coincidence, in one way or another.

She instinctively touched the haunting wound, a souvenir from a lifetime ago. Having gone to great lengths to conceal it, she knew there was nothing left to do but face it.

He took her hand. "You don't have to tell me about it. I just think it's remarkable we've crossed paths before."

She sighed relief. "Good, it was a close call I'd rather not talk about."

"Viktor?"

She nodded. "Not by his gun, just a mission

gone wrong."

"No worries, you're safe with me. Who knows, maybe that's why we were paired up?" He squeezed her hand, and they resumed the ride to Logan Circle.

"Well, here's the piddlee'o tour, short and sweet." Standing in the living room of his rented condo, Lee pointed in an arc from right to left. "T.V. space, dining area, kitchen, laundry closet and my bedroom with full bath, if you want to rinse off."

She followed him there. "My sofa pulls out if you want to sleep separately." He held up his hands like a blackjack dealer. "See? No pervy motives!" He handed her a luxurious towel and a green plaid bathrobe.

"Thanks, I can't wait to wash this food fight off me."

"And to commemorate the day we met..." He held out a Wizards sweatshirt.

"Oh right, I can't believe you remembered that," she marveled with a chuckle.

"I guess you're hard to forget."

She accepted the last item, their fingers touching in the transfer. An electric shiver catapulted through their capillaries. Lee leaned in, drawn to her lips, but she smiled, stepping back to shut the door.

While the water warmed, she spied his medicine chest. It was cliché to pry, and she thought better of it but decided a small peek wouldn't hurt. She could investigate more thoroughly later. Advil, Band-Aids, jock-itch cream, shaving gel, and toothpaste. Nothing suspicious, just run-of-the-mill sundries. She didn't know what she was hoping to find, erectile dysfunction meds maybe. No way the cowboy's campfire was *that* naturally lit.

Swaddled in steam, she closed her eyes, the embarrassment of the evening washing down the drain. Lee seemed to like her goofy side. Maybe she didn't have to try so hard to be perfect. Not that she was. *Far from it.* But she had an image to uphold.

Without it, how would anyone know she meant business?

She chastised herself for giving away the scar. It was a careless move, but the store's heat was blasting, and she was too warm from her workout to wear her coat. Or maybe it was the ants she should be cursing. It was probably just as well. Summer was coming, and she couldn't exactly keep up the turtlenecks, could she?

She emerged from the bathroom sans robe, carrying her balled up outfit. Lee took inventory of her legs accentuated in his large shirt, and led her to the folding doors that housed his stacked appliances. "Voila!" He presented the stain stick, gently cupping it like precious diamonds.

While the wash sloshed, Lee set out the bedding then clattered through kitchen cabinets. "How about a nightcap while we wait. Any of that wine left?"

Tossing cushions on the floor, Gal tugged the hinged contraption, bouncing a bed out of nowhere. "Almost a quarter," she called, peering over the mattress into the picnic basket as Lee eyed her curvy derriere. She arranged the upholstery invitingly on the floor.

"Still holding up?" She poured the refreshment while he offered fresh glasses.

"Yeah, surprisingly. I think it's wearing off." Weight-lifting the goblets, he almost regained half range.

"Whew, I feel so bad about that. Good thing you're athletic. You're the last person I want to poison." She took a drink off his hands and inhaled a long sip.

"Thanks, I'm flattered…I think. So is 'botching' people a habit?" This risky bad-girl side tickled his curiosity.

"Not necessarily, my left Manolo Blahnik is arsenic."

"What?" he nearly choked. "What kind of crazy-ass shoe store do you shop at?"

"Oh, you can't buy these. I devise them myself. You're lucky. I almost wore my lethal Louboutins.

They're literally poison darts—batrachotoxin from the arrow poison frog. I also have Jimmy Choo cyanides and Sergio Rossi ricins."

Lee spat mid-sip. "Calamity Jane! How do you keep them straight? I could've been one fashion misstep from the pearly gates!"

"Don't be so dramatic. The deadly ones have red soles."

"Man, I'd hate to be one of your intended targets," he whistled, downing the rest of his glass. *Or… is that exactly what I am?* Reflecting on the events unfurling since they've met, he realized this could be a real possibility. *That's what I get for fooling around with an assassin,* he smiled. Still, he couldn't deny the arousal her danger provoked.

"I can hardly keep my eyes open," she yawned, shaking the empty bottle. "I think our night is officially capped."

"Yeah, for some reason we haven't gotten much sleep lately," he teased, rising to tidy after their impromptu cocktails. Gal snapped the crisp sheet corners around the mattress, billowing the blanket with a crack of a whip.

They lingered with their good night kiss, finally deciding actual shut-eye was in their best interest.

Galaxy crawled into the sofa bed, directly across from Lee's room. From her vantage point, she watched amused as he dropped trou, revealing muscularly toned thighs and calves.

It occurred to her that most of their ravished moments were in the dark. True, the wildflower sexcapades were in pure daylight, but in the rush, she didn't get a close look at the goods. Now she could enjoy her own private peep show.

Lee stripped off his shirt, revealing brawny pecs. Taking his time, he peeled off his PJ bottoms, giving her a bold eyeful. He turned around to untuck the covers, flexing his glutes for her benefit before climbing into bed.

"Good night," he grinned, snapping off the lamp. Gal blushed and pulled the blanket over her head, embarrassed to be caught drooling.

Awakening first and forgetting where she was, her fight or flight instinct bolted her upright. Squinting at the blurry red numbers blaring across the room, her brain registered 5:11 a.m. The sun would be up soon. The shag carpet tickled her feet as she slowly crept out of bed, feeling her surroundings. The blanket around her waist tried to follow, but resistance tugged her back. Mattress spring snag? Her gaze fell upon the outline of a body instead.

Oh, right. The looming intruder in the middle of the night. It had to be the most pleasurable invasion she'd ever encountered. For a split second, she fought the urge to crawl back in and spoon. But not wanting to risk waking him, she freed herself, eyes adjusting as she tiptoed into the bathroom.

Splashing cold water on her face—*ah, the old Siberian wake-up call*—she knew this was her chance to snoop once and for all. Catching her reflection, she hooted at herself. Oversized sweatshirt, smeared make-up, rat-nest strands. "Should've kept the ponytail," she mused aloud, searching for a brush. Finding one in the last drawer, she was about to run it through her hair when a few leftover strands gave her pause.

Not a good idea leaving evidence behind, but hmm, wouldn't hurt to run a DNA diagnosis, get some info on her partner. Being careful, she unwound the threads, plucking a Puffs Plus and tucking them inside.

She spotted a jar of Noxema in the cabinet above the John and washed her face. Thankfully blessed with a nice complexion, she didn't worry about going without makeup. She rinsed off a comb standing vertically against a corner and unsnarled her tangles. What else did Lee have in here?

Rummaging amongst the shelves, the sight of spermicide short-circuited a brain wave. It hadn't sunk in that he had lovers in his closet and for some reason, it made her jealous. She sat on the seat disheartened. She had divulged the tragedy of Viktor but never asked him about any romantic anguish of his own. Of course, hunky Lee had a past! At least it was just a sample-sized tube, and the important thing was, he was free for her now.

When she pushed the lever down to flush, the jolt vibrated the shelf, causing the aluminum tube to roll off, plop into the bowl and slip away with the vortex. Oh no, water was backing up! Even though it appeared to fit through the opening, it must've stuck sideways along the way.

Quick thinking, even before six in the morning, she yanked the lid off to slam the fluid master down. Whew! In a rush, her hand dislodged something loose and was now bobbing along the tank water. It didn't look like the usual mechanisms. She fished it out, examining it closely.

A thin vial. She rolled it over, managing to read the worn miniature label. *Bombykol*. What the hell was that? She added it to the hair samples, planning to research it later at her desk.

She scrubbed her hands and then brushed her teeth with a toothpasted finger. Wadding the tissue in her fist, she quietly exited the room—"Oomph," right into Lee's rock-hard chest.

"Good morning!" he greeted, amused. "Everything okay in there? I heard clanging."

"Yes, well, sort of. The cabinet rattled, and some ointment fell in. Water started backing up, so I intervened under the lid. Do you have a plunger?" Asking for a toilet tool was the least romantic thing ever.

"Should be under here." He fiddled under the sink, producing an auger. "This should grab it. Like a claw game."

He aimed the wire, bending it under the cavity. "So the door jiggled open, and it just rolled out?"

"Well, I forgot to shut it when I was looking for a comb," she admitted. "I didn't realize it would shake so much."

"Yeah, plumbing is oddly rigged. The owner promised to refurbish this summer." Lee gritted his teeth, wriggling the snake. "A tube fell in? Was it the anti-itch cream? I think that was all I had in there. I get eczema in warm weather," he confessed, revealing just about his only flaw. "Thought that was the cause of my thumb trouble, but it must have been something else." He looked her in the eye, a fleck of mischief flashing in his own. "Tube was almost gone, rolled up pretty good. It might have wedged in tight. I'm surprised it could even get past the outlet."

Gal tried to disguise her guilt. "I didn't see the label. Just a splash, swirl, then poof." Would he be embarrassed if he saw what disappeared? Men didn't seem to mortify as easily, so maybe she should just come clean. She squeezed her hands to brace her nerves, then remembered the evidence in her palm. "I'll go make coffee."

"Great idea. This isn't hooking anything. I think I can reach in and get it, maybe bend the tube manually." He dropped the device and grabbed some gloves from under the sink.

She hurried into the living room, slipped the

crumbled tissue into an eyeglass case, and then dashed into the kitchen to fumble with a coffee filter. She measured a scoop of grounds when she heard the all-clear gurgling and knew Lee would be out any moment.

On the fourth scoop, she felt arms around her waist. "Let's start over with a proper greeting," he nuzzled below her ear.

"Our first sleepover," she agreed, turning around. Kissing revealed his minty breath too.

"Don't worry, that spermicide was old," he murmured into her hair, squeezing her close.

"What?" she asked, bewildered, masking the panic bubbling within.

"You heard me," he chuckled. "I had it pushed back pretty far, behind a box of Q-tips. Doubt it could kamikaze into the can."

Gal forced a laugh, grateful for the good timing of roasted beans. She busied herself pouring, stalling for words.

"I'm surprised cotton swabs weren't splayed

haphazardly on the floor, like pick-up sticks," he bemused with a wink.

"Yeah, a miracle," she offered with the steaming cup. "Do you have any cinnamon? Oh, here it is," she rambled, rummaging through a cabinet. A few spicy sprinkles later, she spat a mouthful into the sink, holding up chili powder to her chagrin.

Lee chuckled, "You don't like your coffee caliente?"

"Very funny, you really should get a spice rack!"

"So you could snoop through that too?" He was only poking fun but noticed her discomfort. "Gal, it's okay. Nothing to hide. No hideous diseases." He kissed her forehead then sipped the overflowing brim. "Are you hungry? I can rustle up an omelet."

She nodded. "Sounds delicious. I'm sorry, my hair looked like a yeti, and I saw a comb—"

Lee waved her off. "It's fine. I used it once, about a year ago. Hated it. Scorched like Hell."

Gal nearly choked on his accurate reference, watching butter sizzle in a pan. "Why did you keep it then?"

"I forgot all about it, to be honest." He whisked eggs and milk, pouring it into the hot skillet, giving it time to set. "I should've chucked it right away, but the woman I was seeing," he paused to make air quotes, "Crazy Kat, believed it was the sure-fire method. She insisted it protected against STIs. But my doctor disagreed. It kills healthy cells too, opens up a chance for viruses. I told her that, but she didn't buy it. So I had to fake it."

"And we girls think we cornered that market."

He shook his head, smiling, chopping onions, bell peppers and ham. "With other methods. When she asked why it no longer burned, I said we must have gotten used to it." He picked up his mug, chuckling into his brew. "She lived with me for a while so I couldn't just toss it out because she looked through the trash, pockets, my briefcase, everything. Talk about trust issues."

"I'll say! Was she justified, if you don't mind me asking?"

"If you're thinking I cheated, no worries there. Like I told you, I don't play that game. But I was working closely with my former partner, Audra Whitman. Kate thought something was up. Never believed me, no matter what I said, the spermicidal maniac! Couldn't stand our undercover stings, but didn't mind being seared by Nonoxynol-9."

"She sounds awful," she sputtered in hysterics, holding her side.

"It gets worse. Audra and I had to pose as husband and wife once, and she went ballistic, blew our case. That's when I ended it, couldn't take it anymore. My partner got torqued and asked for a re-assignment."

"That's a shame." Reaching for a refill, she waved the pot. "I remember Audra."

He held out his cup. "You know her?"

"We worked in the research department a few months before I transferred to you. Friendly, petite, pretty blonde, right? Quite sassy with a southern accent." *Was that a smile widening his jaw?* "Ah, I see how it was," she teased. "Is that why Kate was a jealous hawk?"

"It was all very professional," he protested, bringing the platter of eggs to the table. "I admired her, yes. Like you said, she was fun, kind, lively." He sat, digging into his breakfast. "But it was strictly business."

"Uh-huh, sure, like us?" she grinned, running her foot up his leg.

"*Nothing* like us," he assured, returning the footsy favor. "I may have had an innocent crush, sure, but I was completely faithful to my girlfriend."

Gal snorted into her coffee, making soft bubbles. "What?"

"Don't feel bad, I had a wee crush on her too."

Lee dropped his fork. "What? No way!"

"Well, what's not to like? You said so yourself."

"True, she's a sparkplug. So, did anything happen?" He leaned in, his attention aroused.

"Not what you're thinking. One night, she had enough of my Viktor pity party and insisted on dragging me to a club to cheer me up."

"An outrageous night on the town, huh? She was always up for a good time."

"Yeah, but I wouldn't call it outrageous."

"Really? She had some zany tales about her college days. And she tried getting me to join a flash mob once or twice. What did she get you to do?"

A mischievous smirk blushed her cheeks. "She told me those stories too, so I was leery of going out. I had this nightmarish vision of wet tee-shirt contests in the reflecting pool. Mmm, this is delicious. Have you always been a cook or did you go undercover as a chef?" She jumped up to fetch the coffee pot.

"No contest there. You'd win by a landslide," he laughed, pulling her in by the back of the sweatshirt and plopping her on his lap. "Don't keep me in suspense. Did you end up in jail, a tat parlor? Oh I know, a trapeze park!"

"Not even close," Gal giggled. "Yeah, drunken acrobats, that sounds safe."

"So there *was* something! C'mon, spill. I like a

good story with breakfast."

"Then you should get the morning paper because there's really nothing to tell."

"Your Cheshire grin says otherwise," Lee goaded. "Just knowing you had a girl crush..."

"Tame your wild pony, Cowboy. It wasn't that kind of crush. And she must have mellowed with age, or professionalism because it was just a plain ol' boring girls' night."

"I find that hard to believe. The past few days with you have been anything but dull."

"Okay, but don't say I didn't warn you. Audra was convinced guys fawning all over me would mend my confidence. I severely doubted, having wallowed for weeks in vats of rocky road."

He envisioned chocolate ice cream dripping down her chin, pooling inside her cleavage like a delicious trough. "Yum... I mean, I'd still give you my number."

"Uh huh, sure Schmoozy." She traced his scruffy jaw with both hands and planted a kiss, knowing and feeling full well what he was thinking. "So anyway, I did my best to dress hot and then Audra shows up, a knock-out twenty! Some ego boost, huh?"

She got up to devour her breakfast before it got cold. "So even though I wasn't up for it, I was prepared to fight off gentlemen suitors. And they did swarm—for Audra! That was such a slap. I downed a few shoulders of Guinness, got crabbit as a cat. Somehow she managed to charm them, sending them my way. I wasn't in the mood for her seconds, and they ran for the hills, their bitch radars pinging off the charts. Then being a devoted friend, she doted on me, making sure I was okay."

"Sounds about right. What happened next?" he probed, enchanted by every word.

"Well, to get me over my belly-aching, she told me I was pretty and smart, then pulled me onto the dance floor by my silk scarf." She paused, sectioning her omelet. "Maybe it was the booze or being smushed tight at the bar, but there was a lot of giggling. Do you remember her laugh, that musical chime?"

"Yeah," he mumbled. "Like a magic potion. Could get you to do anything."

Her face tried to hide agreement. "Yeah, it was a fun night. She was right. It helped snap me out of my funk. Do you have any orange juice?" She rose, turning toward the fridge.

"That's it? No antics? There had to be something." He folded his arms, his hard stare wearing her down.

She returned to her seat, burying her face in her hands. "Okay, okay. I can't believe we did this, but we tried smuggling a barrel of peanuts into the National Zoo."

"What? You broke in rolling a whole drum of peanuts? The squirrels must've loved you!"

"Not exactly. The crate wouldn't budge, so we loaded our purses instead. And the break-in was a bust. Bending over the fence, the beer started to protest so you can imagine the only thing making it over. And then what a sight we were! Audra tangled in the chain links, trying to get me down. Even the cabbie helped," she snorted. "Aud even convinced him to drive all the way to my place in Otterbein, then tucked me in and made sure I was comfy."

"Yeah?"

Gal laughed, nudging his foot. "It's not like we had a pillow fight. I was sick. She gave me a ginger ale, crackers and draped a cool cloth over my head. I apologized for spoiling the evening. She said I probably prevented us from being arrested, then invited me lingerie shopping the next day if I was up for it."

"Were you?" he asked eagerly, willing it to happen.

"You can thank her for that pink zebra you like so much. She taught me how to feel beautiful, even when nobody's watching."

Chapter Thirteen

Being romantically involved with Lee made Galaxy's job difficult. Sometimes she forgot she was more than just his lover and LINK partner but an actual Russian assassin. Well, half-Slavic anyway. Driving into work together meant walking into the building with him, which made it tricky to drop off lab samples. What excuse could she give to ditch him?

"See you for lunch? I have to research DNA tests for Fitzy. I told him last night I was a social worker," she chuckled. *Ah, good one, Gal, since you do want to examine the molecular structure of those hairbrush samples.*

"Oh yeah. Fitzy. I almost forgot about him. See how you distract me?"

"Oh!" Gal suddenly remembered, stopping in her tracks. "Speaking of distractions, in all the mess, I forgot to tell you. Come into my office," she motioned, peering down the hall as they came upon her door, not wanting to catch the boss' ire.

"Fitz said his mom, his adopted mother, is the one behind these Kennedy shenanigans. Told him he could walk right in and claim his birthright."

"Yikes," Lee winced. "She sounds cray-cray for Cocoa Puffs. Did he tell you her name?" He nestled into his favorite chair, getting comfortable.

"Let me think. I was the slapstick opening act, right after," she grimaced, mulling it over. "I tell you what. I'll look into it while I'm digging up methods of proof for ol' Fitzy. You go off and do your thang," she shooed. "I can't think with you staring at me."

Lee gave her an odd look. "Okay, I'm going. I'll call Fitz to make another appointment."

Gal almost protested, not wanting to deal with Harold again, but thought better of it. At least he was leaving.

She watched him disappear into his office and close the door. Sighing relief and short on time, she sprinted the specimens to the lab.

"Hey, Andle. How are you today? Can you run these for me?"

She handed the evidence to the technician who was wearing a lab coat over a black *Megadeth* tee shirt, but other than that, no one would have suspected this metal head rocked science with his stylish red frames, goatee and dirty blonde ponytail.

"Sure, you know, anything for you. Casual Thursday? That's a nice change." He nodded at her hip-hugging denim as he examined the contents.

Gal crossed her arms, hoping he didn't spot the faint orange splotch on her elbow she forgot to dab.

"Hair, easy, that'll take seventy-two hours. Bombykol? Where did you find that?"

"Taped inside a toilet tank. You know what it is?"

"Yes, it's a pheromone. From a moth, to be exact. What case are you on?"

"Top secret," Gal smiled, but inside she was seething. "Just let me know about the hair, okay?" Snatching the vial, she dashed to her office and kicked the bottom drawer. Well, this explained everything! Fuming, she nursed her toes, recalling his niceness, all that chivalry. Was it all a front? Obviously, he was honey-trapping right back!

How did he pull it off? Was he slipping the stuff into her coffee, massaging it into her skin that generous first night? Or was he dabbing it behind his ears, letting the chemicals woo her? Did he not trust her? Of course not, she had revealed too much.

Well, this just made things easier. Finally, she could separate herself and get back to the operative. All she had to do was pull off the Best Actress award. Did she have it in her?

To get her mind off Lee, she dove into research for Fitz. He was making a great smokescreen after all, and she did want to help him. If he had rights to the Kennedy name and fortune, they shouldn't get away with snuffing him out. Hmm, what was *that* name? She really did forget. She rubbed her temples and closed her eyes, imagining the stunts the night before.

"Franny Cooper!"

Gal's head shot up. "Yes, that's it. Oh, Lee, when did you pop in?"

"Just now. Do you have a headache?" He patted his pockets. "I think I have some aspirin."

"No, just trying to think." *As if I'd take anything you offered from now on.* "How'd you figure it out?"

"I was booking Harold's walk, and it dawned on me. Hey clod, just ask him. Told him Gail was looking into DNA testing and forgot his mother's name." He held up his phone. "So I searched it. Came up with tons of Franny Coopers but none that fit our case, not that we have much to go on."

"Ah, brilliant. Do you think he's lying?"

"His story's beginning to fall apart, don't you think? Why race off if you're innocent?"

"Yeah, it seems shifty alright, but what do we know? Maybe he has some kind of post traumatic thing. He sounded genuine last night. Hey, what about adoption records? Or maybe JFK kept a diary."

"Good thinking! Maybe it's shelved in a special section of the library. We should make a pit stop

there. Or, maybe he hid one in the floorboards at ol'
1600. What do you say, up for getting lost again?" He
raised a suggestive eyebrow, then added reminders
to his phone.

"Sure!" Gal tried to sound flat and casual but
there was something tantalizing about that place,
their place, she couldn't refuse. She watched his eyes
fall on the vial, so she placed a manila folder over it,
but it was too late.

"What do you have there?"

She tossed it at him. "You tell me."

"Bomb-y-kol?" he read, puzzled. "What is it? A
new DNA solution for cheek swabs?"

"You can drop the innocent act," she snapped, a
little sharper than she meant to.

Lee was genuinely baffled. "Bomb-
whatchamacallit? I'm feeling a little bomb-shelled
right now by your bombastic mood. Is it almost that
time of the month or something?" It slipped out
before he could lasso it back in and he braced himself
for the dust storm sure to follow.

"You men like to blame everything on that, easy peasy, one stop shopping. Like guys don't have mood swings of your own."

"I'm sorry, that was insensitive of me. But if that's *not* it, is that the problem then?" *Oops...* "You know, we haven't exactly been careful." He was at her side for support.

That gave Galaxy reason to stop and count, and she was annoyed at the detour. "I don't know, it's only been three days, but it was clear to me from the start *that* ball was in my court. Nice try, changing the subject, Black Bart." Her brain was on spin cycle. Had it only been a few days?

"I didn't mean to. Tell me why you're mad." He rubbed her arm. It was a relief to hear about the birth control, though. He vowed to be more vigilant.

"Oh no, you don't! Are you applying more of this on me right now?" She jerked her arm away.

"I honestly don't know what you're talking about."

"So you have no idea how this got inside your

toilet tank? I accidentally knocked it loose when I fiddled with the fluid master." Her sarcasm was giving him a cavity.

"*My* toilet? No way. Scout's honor, I don't know what that is!" It was creeping him out. "Is it a bomb? No, that can't be, or it would've gone off. Right now I'm wishing it was truth serum because I'd like to know what's going on."

"That makes two of us. It's pheromone. You used it to make me fall in love with you! Of all the slimy—"

"I did not!" His words cut sharp. "How do I know you didn't use it on me so I'd fall in love with you?"

They stood there for the first time openly suspicious of one another. It was very unsettling, not to mention heart-breaking. Just as the sting subsided, they realized what they had just confessed. They were about to address it when Andle poked his head in.

"Gal, preliminary results from the hair samples

show mix results, but one is matching international art thief, Katjarina Kreskinova."

Gal gasped, pale as a ghost, turning to Lee. "What were you doing sleeping with Viktor's wife?"

Chapter Fourteen

If the air in Galaxy's office wasn't tense enough, it now practically sparked.

"*Viktor's* wife? No, I didn't! I don't even know Viktor, much less his wife."

"Who's Viktor?" Andle wanted to know.

"Well, her hair didn't walk in by itself," Gal pouted.

"What do hair samples have to do with me?" He knew he sounded defensive, but they had him cornered. And why was a lab guy questioning him?

"I took them from a brush in your bathroom." The sun blared appropriately between the open slats, blinding her as she awaited the interrogation.

Lee stood there, speechless.

Andle turned to Clancy. "What was Katjarina doing at your place?"

"I'm wondering the same thing!" Gal glared.

"My place? She wasn't. And for land's sake Galaxy, unbelievable! What else did you swipe?"

"Just the two," she said, the slow swivel of her chair matching her glum mood. She glanced at Andle. "One set must be Lee's."

"Well, there's two kinds all right, but the other is synthetic. An auburn hairpiece I'm guessing?"

They both stared at Lee, arms crossed.

"I didn't have any wig-donning sleepovers at my place if that's what you're thinking. And I certainly haven't harbored any art wranglers. You're not even hundred percent positive the hair is hers. How can it possibly match without a comparison?" His voice was escalating into a flabbergasted falsetto. None of this made sense.

"In my experience," Andle began, turning to Gal, trying to impress her with his expertise, "and that's a lot," before spinning back to Lee, "early indicators usually prove true. And we do have her sample in the database. We nabbed a strand off an old George Washington painting at the White House.

An attempted robbery foiled, probably because it's so large."

The agents' eyes locked long enough to acknowledge the location before turning away.

"*Usually?* So still a chance it could be wrong," Lee smugged. "I'll take those odds. I also happen to know that you have a better chance of collecting mitochondrial DNA rather than individual nuclear DNA since whole follicles are rare, especially in a brush where hair is prone to breakage. So at best, you can *maybe* narrow it down to a general family. And don't get me started on the chemicals in hair dye these days."

The stunned scientist shrugged. "Sure, if you want to look at the glass as half empty, but this one is overflowing with—Wait a minute, if you're so innocent, how did you know Katjarina's hair was dyed?"

The stares were back, perspiration now seeping through his shirt. "I didn't! I was just spitting facts. You hardly ever get the real deal these days." He nodded at Galaxy's streaks for exhibit A.

"Well, even with the bleach, the root was intact so—"

"You got lucky."

Gal watched the testosterone tennis match in fascination, not sure who was winning.

With not much else to say, the trio squirmed uncomfortably and at that moment, held hostage by silence, Lee wanted to be anywhere but there. "The reality is, I came in here to help you, Gal, not stumble into a lion's den and get eaten alive." He started to leave, but Andle was still in the doorway.

"Sure, disappear when the collar gets hot, but you're all over me when other things heat up!"

The lab tech's eyebrows shot up in surprise.

Lee turned around. "It's such a warm feeling, isn't it, Gal? We're supposed to have each other's back."

"You call that having each other's back?" she huffed.

"Look, I've never met this Katjarina. Maybe she

lived there before me. Did you think of that? That vial must be hers too. Or who knows, maybe it's even Kate's or my landlord's."

"Wait, are you talking about that Bombykol? Doesn't work on humans. Only on silkworm moths." Andle chuckled, glad to know something Lee did not, relieved to dispel the discomfort in the room.

That caught Gal's interest. "It doesn't?"

"No," he laughed. "Unless it's mind over matter, like lucky jock socks or something. But scientifically, it's useless on us."

"Why didn't you tell me that before? You can't just drop the word pheromone and not expect me to freak."

Now Andle was under the heat lamp. "Sorry, but you grabbed it and split. I didn't get a chance."

Gal nodded thoughtfully. "Oh, yeah, right." She took a cleansing breath. "We'll, thanks, Sir, you've been a big help. If we find anything else, we'll be sure to bring it your way." She rose, gently shoving him out and closing the door.

Dumped in the hall like a bag of garbage. What was going on with those two? Andle was envious. If only pheromones *did* work, he'd slather some on and have a hearty helping of Galaxy himself.

Inside the room, Lee noticed she still looked frazzled, more so than before Andle popped in. "Are you okay?"

She leaned against the door. "No. It's a dirt move to control someone without their knowledge. I know you said you didn't," she rushed to add when she sensed his protest. "And Andle claims it's futile, but it's still unnerving."

"You're right. I'm spooked too, especially since it's been in *my* apartment this whole time. I can see where you jumped to that conclusion. Makes me wonder if I was under the influence. Kate was a crackpot, ya know?" He whistled relief, glad to be free of *that*.

"Yeah, that's another thing. How could you sleep with Katjarina? Of all the women in the world, after I spilled my guts to you… "

"I didn't—"

"You promised I could trust you!"

"Oh, really, you want to talk about trust?"

"You're right. Stealing evidence is the same thing as sleeping with your mortal enemy, plunging a knife into my heart and cranking it like a wind-up toy." She sat down, tossed a folder from one corner to another and sighed. "Maybe the real issue is you with other women."

"You're kidding, right? I had a life before we met. Same as you."

"I know, it's insane," she admitted. "I'm not saying it makes sense. Just like you disappearing every Monday from lunch time on. What are you doing at the Montessori school? Do you have a kid there or are you moonlighting on another case behind my back? I know it's not softball practice or your nephew's district." *Oops.* Her eyes fell on her bracelet. *Quick, blame the derma-transmitter so he doesn't think you're a stalker.*

"Ah, is that why my schedule's missing?" he

grinned, no longer startled by her sly stunts. "If you want to know anything, just ask. You don't have to trail me or use your sticky fingers behind my back. What creeps me out, is a criminal prowling around my place! But I didn't sleep with one." He grabbed a handful of hard candy from the dish and sunk into the chair.

"I said I was sorry. And I thought I just did. You have to admit the hair speaks for itself." She twirled a piece of her own, resisting the urge to chew it. "Unless you have a habit of using old brushes left by previous tenants."

"We don't even know they're hers. I started out in the CIA lab before hitting the field, and I know it's tricky getting the right part of the hair follicle for accuracy, not to mention environmental factors affecting the specimen."

"Ah, I thought you were just trying to throw Andle off his game. I didn't have you pegged as a lab rat. CIA, huh? Well, I hope you're right." She sat down. "Hey, what's Kate's last name? Sounds too coincidental both women are named Kat."

"Zucker, not Kresky-whatever you said, so there!"

"Hmm, interesting. Did you know Zucker means 'thief' in German? Just saying…"

"I thought your crook was Russian," Lee countered. "There's no way she was Katjarina. I would have noticed something."

"Like a wig or the scorching pain tolerance?" Gal gave him an obvious look, pelting a peppermint his way. "Think, McSpy! It has to be the same woman. Her DNA is practically in your bathroom. Did she use that Bombykol on you too?" She was half-joking but what if Andle was wrong and it did alter people, rendering them brainless zombies in the process?

"There's no way she wore a wig. I've seen her swim laps. It's probably just a fluke that she was a ginger, but the carpet matched the drapes. Plus I've yanked her hair plenty of times!"

Gal's horrified look prodded him to explain.

"She liked it rough, sorry." He was leaning back on the upholstery, free-throwing balled-up wrappers into a waste basket. The crumpled cellophane was too light, fluttering down before reaching the can. "No NBA for me," he murmured, dissecting recent relationships. Were *any* of them real?

"Maybe it was glued to a swim cap. Or a weave."

They simmered in silence for a few seconds. "Hey, if that stuff *was* effective, wouldn't it make the perfect trap? Lure away museum guards or something."

"I guess. If you're a moth." She spun around in frustration then stirred up a thought. "Did Kate work at one?"

"No, an intern at the Library of Congress." He aimed one more candy wrapper, but it caught the air draft and drifted sideways. "Can't get much duller than that."

"Well, libraries are kind of like museums. We might need to revisit that later. What case were you working on when she blew your cover?"

"Nothing artsy. We were busting an illegal adoption ring. Hey!" He slid up straight, deciding to test her loyalty. "Suppose she was in on it?"

"Kate? I'm sure of it. That scene she made was probably a diversion."

"No, I mean Audra. She got all huffy and quit suddenly. Maybe it was staged."

"Why would you think that? She's so sweet. Genuinely kind to everyone."

"Still crushing?" he teased. "C'mon, no one is *that* perfect! Have you seen her around lately? I haven't and to tell you the truth, I'm not feeling too trusting about anyone right now."

"No, not in a while." Gal looked down, doodling with her pen. She had almost told him *he* was that perfect. What if he was right and he wasn't either? "This discovery is throwing us for a loop. If you want to call off our dancing date, I understand. I'll be bummed, but I can handle it." What an understatement! Even though the short-lived affair had to end sometime, she knew he would be hard to get over.

"Don't be silly. We're in this together." There was no way he was letting her out of his sight now. Whether or not they remained romantic, he needed to keep her close. "C'mon, we have to get the dog, talk with Fitz. Let's not get away from our job."

Gal nodded, feeling a little better. She grabbed her purse, remembering she hadn't finished her research. "Argh, I still have to find a place to run his DNA."

"I'm surprised you didn't pull a piece of *his* hair."

"There's a plan! Would it even tell us anything, like that family factor you mentioned?"

"It's worth a try since we don't have anything else to go on. If we're lucky, maybe there'll be some wild strands in his hoodie. And what about testing it right here? Andle seems qualified, despite his ability to rush to conclusions."

"Too close to home. You think he can be

discreet? We can't let Geoff find out."

"I've seen the puppy way he pants at you, Gal. I have a feeling he'll do whatever you want. Let's grab a cheek kit too while we're at it. Onto the yellow brick road," Lee gestured. They headed toward the lab. "Special Olympics."

"Where?" Bewildered, she looked around for a poster or donation box.

"That's where I go every Monday. I help a little brother train for the summer games. We practice in the gym."

"Aw, that's so sweet. But I thought your family lived near Houston?"

"Not a sibling, we met at the Big Brothers program. So no worries, okay? No secret kids if that's what's bugging you and no, I'm not double-dipping as an undercover teacher, although I did do that once." He held the door open for her. "Evan has Downs and is a sports nut so when he expressed interest in basketball, I started coaching."

Gal's heart melted. "That is the noblest thing I

ever heard."

Lee was embarrassed. "Hey, it's not like I'm a king or anything. I just blow a whistle and give pep talks. The kids are the real heroes."

Chapter Fifteen

"I can't believe he was a no show!" Lee fumed against the backdrop of honking traffic and bus exhaust, pacing Harold along the sidewalk near the park. It was a rare hot day in early May, so Gal cupped her hand to make an impromptu water bowl while Lee poured from his sports bottle. The sheepdog's tongue tickled her palms.

"Maybe we should've swapped," Gal suggested, wiping her hands on her jeans." She tousled Harry's fur anyway. *Maybe he's growing on me.*

"We went out of our way to pick up the pup. Does he think we like hollering down an empty well?" He looked at his phone and sighed.

"He doesn't know that," Gal reminded. "For all he cares, we live in the city. What if something happened to him?"

"Like what, runaway dogs?"

"Or playing statue in a secret staircase." She raised a mysterious eyebrow.

"You think?"

"Hey, maybe he got lucky last night." She brightened at the sight of the bakery across the street. "I'll run over and ask around for Sarah. Maybe they have iced coffee."

"Better than broiling out here. Good luck. I'll walk Harold around the block."

He strolled leisurely, watching her jaywalk. *Always the rebel*. A longing ached his heart. *Are we over?* If they could just restart their day. But how could that be when she packed poison and kept pocketing his things. At least now he didn't feel so bad about sending someone over to sweep her place while she slept at his.

Harold's barking drew attention to a white delivery van skidding around the corner, barely missing Gal as she reached the curb and entered the shop.

A little bell tinkled over the door, which fit the fairy-like interior of The Affectionary Confectionary. A tiny cinnamon-haired brunette with matching freckles and an appropriate pixie cut tended the counter. "Hello," she greeted, her diminutive voice matching her stature, the aroma of fresh cake inviting her in.

"Hi, do you have iced coffees, Sarah?" Gal asked, incorporating her name tag, a trick she learned from Lee.

"Not officially. The sweltering day took us by surprise. I haven't made the concentrated syrup yet, but I can make you a single with an expresso."

"Great, can I trouble you for two? My boyfriend's waiting outside."

"Sure, take a look at our fresh bakery case while you wait. I made cherry cheesecake croissants. They're going fast." Sarah scooped ice into two tall smoothie cups.

"I like your towering cupcakes. I know someone who's a fan."

Sarah laughed. "Yeah, they're pretty popular with birthday parties. Do you have kids?"

"It's our dog walker, Fitz. Do you know him?"

The pastry chef's smile faded, and she set down the creamer. "Only as a customer," she squirmed, then leaning over the counter, whispered, "Is he well?"

"He's a little off," Gal admitted. "But he's pretty harmless." At least she hoped. "Why, has he been acting strange?"

"Always, but maybe he's just the nervous type. He's here every day for the daily special, but yesterday he asked me if he upped his game, and bought a fancy three-tiered cake, would I go out with him? He wouldn't take no for an answer, so I gave in and met him at the park last night for a movie. And then…" she glanced around, feeling foolish. "He kept bragging about Marilyn Monroe being his mother. Gave me the creeps. I left early, thankful I had to start baking at 2 a.m." The beeping of the register tallied the order.

Gal leaned forward and looked around. "Did you get that Norman Bates feeling?" She was glad to put her new pop culture to use.

Sarah's brown eyes widened, confirming solidarity. "Yes, now that you mention it, that's exactly what it was."

"Did you know they're playing that movie next week at the park?"

Sarah shivered. "I hope he doesn't ask me to go." They shared an uneasy laugh. "Here, have a cupcake on the house. Fitz didn't come by yet for his. I think I hurt his feelings. If you see him, tell him I'm sorry."

"Thank you, I sure will. We've been waiting for him over an hour but nary a shadow. Do you know where he lives?"

"No, sorry. But he seemed obsessed with the White House for some reason. Maybe he camps near there?"

"We noticed that too. Well, thanks again." Gal started to leave, then backtracked. "You know, it really might be true. We're looking into it."

"What? That he's insane?" She spilled the napkins she was stuffing into the holder.

"No, that he's a Kennedy," Gal winked, nodding goodbye.

Outside in the heat, she spotted Lee and the slobber monster sitting inside a bus shelter. "She met him at the park last night, but got scared off and left." Holding out the cardboard caddy, he helped himself to drink, peeling a straw for her.

"That's too bad. I haven't seen him anywhere around either." Harold tried jumping up to sniff the plastic domed treat. "What are you going to do with that?"

"I don't know, food fight?" Wincing, she got an ice-cracking brain freeze. "It was on the house. Maybe your nephew will like it? Or better yet, we can bribe Fitz if we ever find him. Sarah seemed to think he was hovering close to the Prez. Did you call him back?"

"Yeah, no answer. Do you think he might have

done something foolish, like get arrested?" They headed back to the car. "Maybe he left town early. I saw a suspicious van with Smithsonian plates. It almost hit you."

"Yeah, that was crazy close. Do you think someone short was in the driver seat?"

"Harold started barking. Maybe he recognized him, or maybe he was just protecting you. Dogs have a sixth sense."

"Aww, Hairy. You are a sweet pom-pom, aren't you?" She ruffled his fur. "But why would he leave when he knew we were going to test his DNA?"

"Exactly. Doesn't something smell rotten here?"

"Yeah, you're so right!" Gal stopped in her tracks, pointing at Harold.

After disposing of the doggie scrap bag, they squeezed Hal once again into the Mustang. "Should we ride over and see if we can find him? Maybe we should track down Franny Cooper while we're at it. They could be together."

A convoy of cop cars whizzed past, and they

noticed the public in a tizzy.

"What's going on?" Lee revved the engine, snapping on the radio.

"*—also known as the Jacqueline Kennedy Garden, during preparations for the Mother's Day Tea. Traffic is being diverted at this time. No suspects have been identified, and terrorism has been ruled unlikely. Stay tuned to WDC ROX, the Capitol's Classic Rock for the latest details. We repeat, an explosion in the East Garden of the White House—*"

"Follow them," Gal signaled as he stepped on the gas. "I hope our boudoir isn't ruined." For a minute she felt sentimental, forgetting she was miffed at Lee's seductive swindle. Their phones lit up simultaneously, so Gal answered for the both of them.

"Yes, Geoff, we just heard. We're already downtown. Yep, we're heading over to investigate. Roads are closed, but we'll get there somehow." She disconnected, feeling warm panting in her ear as Harold dribbled out the window. "Why do we always have the drool master in tow when we need a quick getaway?"

The dog wagged his backside in response.

Lee tailgated the police, snaking his way through traffic cones until they pulled into the rear entrance of the White House gate.

An officer walked over. "You can't be here. You'll have to turn around."

Gal flashed her badge. "We're on this case."

He nodded. "That's an unorthodox bomb sniffer you have there, but he won't be necessary. We have our K-9 unit. It appears the damage is limited to the grounds, but we'll take Raj for a look around." The cops and the German shepherd disappeared through a service door.

They looked at the sheepdog, ruffling his fleece. "Be a good boy and stay," Lee chuckled, tossing him a biscuit.

Walking around the premises to survey the garden, gobs of frosting and cake chunks adorned the rose bushes and topiaries. The linen chair backs were smudged with fudge, ambushed by the flying marble confection.

They found Anita and Tom inspecting a disfigured daffodil display. Police units were scrutinizing the lawns while the cleaning crew waited in the wings.

"The work of a decadent detonator," Gal whispered.

Lee snickered before addressing the media team. "What happened, a pie fight gone awry?"

Anita shook her head. "Well, the suspect is certainly a clown. We're lucky it was just an exploding cake."

"And not during the tea. Hi, I'm Tom Feliz. I'd shake your hands but…" He held up a busted bucket and pieces of its lid. "Liquid nitrogen. Sorry to have missed you the other day."

"Likewise. I'm Galaxy, this is Lee. So you know who the vandal is then? Seems like someone was sending a message," Gal observed.

"Message received," Anita sighed, annoyed.

"Is this related to the previous threats?" Lee asked.

Tom looked at Anita. "We believe so. Guess we have no choice but to cancel the luncheon, especially after receiving that call about power interruption tomorrow."

"What call? Did you trace the line?" Lee asked, concerned.

"Of course. It appears to be legit, automated by PEPCO for a 3 a.m. kill while they update transformers."

"We have generators, but we aren't taking any chances," Anita explained.

"It does sound suspicious. Hey, what size cake was it?" Gal asked suddenly.

"What does that matter? Except for the size of the mess," Lee wondered, looking around.

"A twelve inch tapered three tier. Not quite enough for our guest list."

"Do you have the box it came in? We can trace it back to the bakery, find out who ordered it," Gal suggested.

Anita shook her head. "The cake was delivered directly to the garden on a cart, a day earlier than expected. We don't use a bakery. A woman comes in and does incredible creations for us, right here on the premises. Oh, she works in your building. Francine Bach. She's an old friend, been our special cake provider for years. You don't think she's a suspect, do you?"

"No, I know her as well," Gal said. "I didn't realize she had a side business."

"It's possible the explosion is separate from the bakery source," Lee suggested.

Tom nodded in agreement. "I was thinking the same thing. I'm sure the cake is a dummy since it arrived early. We're having the surveillance footage checked now."

Just then an officer approached, a fistful of wires sprouting from his palm. "Looks like they cut the cameras. You're lucky, no other damage is apparent. This was most likely a warning."

"Thanks, Max. We're beefing up security." Anita glared at Tom.

"On it." Nodding adieu, he sprinted off to inform the National Security Council.

"We'll look into the leads. Thanks for your time," Galaxy promised. On the walk back to the car, she gazed at the portico. "Too bad we can't sneak inside and start searching for that diary."

"I know, I wish we could since we're already here and all. But we can't leave Harold much longer." Lee unlocked the car. Climbing in, he nearly had a conniption. "Holy Avatar!"

Gal was about to sit when she noticed the interior splotched with blue frosting, and then to her horror, so was the dog.

"That damn cupcake!" Lee scowled. "Why didn't you throw it out?'

"I forgot all about it." She tore open a dozen wet wipes, going to town on the headliner and seats.

Lee tackled Hal's fur, but icing and moist crumbs matted in clumps. "I hope my sister has a good groomer."

When they cleaned what they could, only smearing it in the process, Lee headed for Alexandria, peeved. "And I need a good detailer. Not a good day for cake!"

"I thought it was safe in the container. I'll pay for the damage but can we agree Fitzy is the culprit today? Sarah told me he ordered a fancy number yesterday instead of his usual special, upping the ante for a date."

"Weird, especially for a lowly dog walker. And that van peeling away was suspicious! I wish I got a good look at the driver. I think there was a male passenger too. And your lunch lady friend—I bet she's Franny! Seems like an awful coincidence and she fits the age bracket."

"Yeah, I didn't know she had connections to the White House. Sounds like a perfect way in. Now that we got her full name, we can search it."

"And hearing Anita's complaint about Fitz's bomb threat in the first place. It all adds up."

Chapter Sixteen

The dizzying pattern of the parquet floor whirled in and out of view as they waltzed around the ballroom. Lee's mind seemed to have fled, but his feet were painfully present.

Gal flinched until she couldn't stand it any longer. She tapped his shoulder. "Still mad?"

"Oh, sorry," he mumbled, snapping out of his daze. "It just pisses me off. I keep going over it in my head."

"Fitz, my snooping, or the messy Mustang?" she cringed, not sure she wanted to know.

"All of the above, but mostly Fitz. If he was fake, why waste our time with all that DNA nonsense?" They whisked a rounded corner. "Something keeps bugging me. He's a diversion for something but what?"

"Speaking of bugs, whatever happened to that

Urdu lead? That seemed to fall off a cliff."

"Oh, right. The convention left town. Nothing more than peace talks after all. I wired the undersides of the tablecloths, so I guess those got washed. And Anita's phone has been oddly quiet ever since the blast. I should be hearing every conversation she has in her office, including phone calls. Do you suppose she found the device?"

"Police and bomb squad swept every inch of the place yesterday. They had to have confiscated it." The music ended, and they clapped politely with the crowd, heading toward their table to catch their breath.

"Of course, why didn't I think of that? Oh yeah, probably because my car looked like the inside of a frosting can," he teased. "Well, the good part is, I suppose the device will blend in as evidence." They sat out the next dance, a jazzy rendition of *In the Mood*.

Gal guzzled champagne, sighing at the irony as Lee tinkered with his smartphone. "How's your triceps?"

"Practically good as new, thanks. Hey, so Francine checked out. Widowed. Husband retired Navy then stayed in the area as a deputy project manager. Two kids the conventional way. The closest thing adopted was a springer spaniel. Oh, and a Belgium exchange student."

"Are you sure Fitz isn't Belgian?"

"Not unless his real name is Geerta Van Den Smet."

Sharing a chuckle, she smugged, "Good, I knew Francine was too nice to be shady."

"What about Sarah? They did find a flap of her woodland green box under a rose bush, so it does seem to be her handiwork. Maybe she's an accessory. Did she seem sketchy?"

"No, she was adorable. Why would she jeopardize her business? Besides, Sarah voluntarily disclosed all her order logs to police." Gal didn't want to talk about work, so she tried to play footsy. Lee shifted his legs, mistaking her cue as a sign that his were in the way. She sighed, chin in hand, hoping they would be more touchy-feely. This was supposed to be their romantic night after all, but it seemed more like a business deal.

"Watch out for the elephant," she warned, swirling a finger around the rim of her glass, making it moan a haunting hum.

Lee looked confused then regretful. "I was stepping all over your feet, wasn't I?"

"Yes, but that's not what I meant." She submerged her lips in champagne, and the words became a muffled mouthful. When he questioned her with a befuddled frown, she continued. "Look," she said, setting down the drink. "This is our big date, and normally we'd be all over each other. We might as well be in different time zones."

"Yeah, you're right," he sighed, glad it was finally out in the open. "Yesterday was the first time we didn't spend together—I missed you," he added quickly, in case he insulted her with what he was about to say. "But it was also a relief because I needed a breather. I could tell you did too, after that confrontation in your office."

"Yes, we needed time to think. Our relationship flipped from partners to lovers so fast, and it's been intense ever since. I'm not objecting. It's been really hot. But then the Bombykol..."

"Exactly. We went from zero to sixty then jarred to a screeching halt. I think what we're feeling is whiplash." He stared spellbound at the sparkling bubbles climbing his glass. "Now we need to decide if we should let it end us or if we're strong enough to overcome it. The other day, we admitted something pretty wonderful. Do you still feel that way?" He saw sadness in her eyes, but perhaps a speck of love if he wasn't mistaken. Or maybe this was just a hot and heavy one week stand.

"I'm not sure. I can't help thinking the reason we aren't pawing each other now is because the pheromones aren't in the picture."

He took a swig of bubbly. "Was it all jaded? Yeah, that crossed my mind too, but I'm hoping that's not true. Unless Andle was right, and it works on a mind over matter basis. Or lack thereof, in our case." He raised his hand. "I solemnly swear my innocence on the state of Texas. Can you say the same?"

"Sure, I can swear on the state of Texas," she bantered, still tracing the edge of her glass.

"Swear on *your* homeland, or it doesn't count," he chuckled. He caressed her hand. "I'm not sure what role that stuff played with us, but I do know I'm not ready for it to end yet. If at all. Are you?"

The band started an upbeat *Samba.*

Gal closed her eyes, the gesture also a test of touch. Was there anything left between them? His thick hands usually made her swoon, his virility tripping her switch. Detecting the faint pulse of her thumping heart, she knew the monster was alive, if only just barely!

Lee felt it too. "Is this a good sign? Or is it the beat?" He stood, pulling her onto the dance floor to *Baila Casanova* made famous by Paulina Rubio.

This time Lee's feet frolicked in flirtatious form.

Gal enjoyed the twirling tease, their bodies mingling for an instant before being drawn into a pirouette.

"I never told you what a beautiful goddess you are tonight," Lee said when she was back in his arms a few seconds later.

Gal smiled, glad he liked the satin Athena style accentuating her curves, but before she could respond, she was extended, outstretched within his reach.

The glint of sequins caught her eye, and she noticed some women wore shorter dresses with fringe that shimmied with the motion. Even some of the men were decked in Latin flair in form-fitting slacks and bedazzled tops with open chests.

Ballroom dancing used to be more proper. Maybe she should've dressed for flirty fun, but she didn't want to attract too much attention so she chose demure over glitz. Her ecru gown had a subtle gold floral pattern cascading down the bodice with a gilded spacer belt, and at least the side slit added an enticing element. Plus the folds in the fabric doubled as secret inside pockets.

Back in his arms, she admired his classic black and white tuxedo and couldn't help smiling at his turquoise pocket square. "Thanks, you're dapper yourself." *Then again, you always are.*

When Lee dipped her at the end of the number, her heart quickened. Not only because of their sensual duet but because upside down, she thought she saw someone sinister by the punch bowl.

She excused herself to powder her nose. Her motive was artificial—she thought she had spotted Viktor hovering near the hors d'oeuvres. *What was the cad doing here?* If he was back in the states, he was up to no good. She was sure he was there to step on her toes. Scanning the area around the buffet table, and only spotting the regular ballroom crowd, she darted off behind the scenes.

Nothing was amiss. Gal almost expected to see him crouching on the catwalk, hiding amid curtain pulls, sandbags and ropes.

A faded memory came into focus... *Stanislavsky*

Theatre, fifteen years ago, practicing for their first mission together. He was mentoring, eight years older, training her at the tender age of twenty-two, before becoming involved romantically two years later...

But everything here was clearly in order. She checked the restrooms for good measure, sustaining odd looks from several men, and a business card from another when she peeked inside.

Had she hallucinated? Was the mere mention of Katjarina triggering flashbacks, or had she had too much to drink? She supposed it could have been anyone since lots of men were her height with long black hair, high foreheads and trimmed goatees that framed their rugged handsomeness. If only she got a closer look, she could identify the unmistakable scar across his right cheekbone — left by the pear-shaped prongs of her three-carat ring when he broke off their engagement. And that missing right earlobe would be a dead giveaway — damage done by a Siberian wolf four years ago while in hiding. He had proudly killed it and mounted it as a trophy in his cabin.

She ladled what she hoped was virgin punch and surveyed the ballroom. If he wasn't here, why was her mind playing games? Maybe she wasn't over her first love after all. Was anyone? She sipped, tapping her foot to the post-World War II jazz melody.

Arms quietly wrapped around her waist. "Parched?"

Startled, the cocktail splattered on the floor, spraying a random red design on the hem of her gown.

"Didn't mean to spook you," Lee apologized, blotting the puddle with his pocket square. He straightened. "Everything okay? I didn't crunch your toes again, did I?"

Gal smiled. "No, you're a gallant dancer."

As proof, Lee broke out in exaggerated, absurd gestures, matching the schizophrenic beat of trumpets and drums, even imitating a sax player. When the piece ended, he wiped his brow and scooped punch of his own. "Spiked?" he offered with a devilish grin.

Gal nodded, eyes wide, giving him a wary expression. "You're a loon."

"Just trying to impress you with my sax appeal."

She smiled, shaking her head.

"Hey, just loosening things up. You're so serious. What's wrong? I thought we were reconnecting back there."

"No, we were. It's not you. It's just that... I thought I saw Viktor."

It was Lee's turn to look guarded. *Him again?*

"I know, it's crazy, but if he's prowling around, something is very wrong."

"Where did you see him?" He plucked a mini éclair from a doily. The band started Marc Anthony's *Dimelo* as the *Cha-Cha* began.

"Here, by the refreshment table."

Lee eyed the treat, having second thoughts. "I hope he wasn't poisoning anything."

"That's not his style. He's more of an explosives kind of guy."

"Well, that makes me feel better," he huffed, tossing the sweet into the waste bin anyway. "I think we should do a perimeter check."

"I suppose you're right. You never know with villains." She took his cup and swept all the goodies in the trash as a plump woman approached a pastry.

"Hey, I wanted that," she protested.

"We're doing you a favor," Lee began, but she misunderstood and slapped his face.

"Ma'am, these treats have been compromised," Gal explained. When she still looked cynical, Galaxy whispered, "Rat infestation." The woman hurried away appalled, apologizing profusely to Lee.

"You deserved that," she giggled.

"Are you sure it was even him?" He rubbed his cheek.

"Well...not entirely. I *was* upside down."

"Oh geez," Lee grimaced. "Really?" He was already pouring a red river into the plastic lined pail.

"Sorry, but my vibes usually mean something. We should still check around."

"Women's intuition will kill me yet," he muttered, following her to their table.

Gal gave the description they needed. "We'll cover more ground if we split up," she suggested, concealing her compact gun in the creases of her dress.

"Will you be alright? You were distraught by just the idea of him. Take your cell so we can communicate."

She was in the process of tucking it in already and held it up.

"Not taking your purse?"

"A clutch is too cumbersome."

"Well, good thing you have breasts then."

An hour later they slunk into the ballroom looking beat, Gal lugging her strappy heels, Lee's tie unknotted. The band was at the tail end of the sexy number, *Suit and Tie*, by Timberlake and Jay Z.

"Not a trace. Any luck?" Lee inquired, pulling out her chair as they returned to their table.

"Nope, I'm sorry for the wild goose chase. I owe you one." She emptied her pleats, refilling her purse.

"I think we're even. I wrecked your dress."

She examined the bottom quarter edge. "That's okay. I have an excellent dry cleaner."

"Lucky, mine's mediocre."

She chuckled. "I feel bad for destroying the desserts, though."

"They replenished everything. See, everyone's happy."

"Including us?" She reached out and stroked his arm.

"I think this is our song." He stood, inviting her to a slow body meld to *Lady in Red*.

They enjoyed the closeness, amused at their inside joke.

"I missed our mingling," Lee uttered, the deep vibrations taking the edge off.

"Me too," she admitted, closing her eyes against

his shoulder, the safe feelings returning.

"You know, I've been thinking, and now I'm sure pheromones were working their magic on us."

Gal lifted her head, tightening her jaw. "You've got to be kidding me!"

"We emit our own natural chemicals, right? That should've occurred to me during our fight."

She exhaled in relief. "That's true. I guess we both got defensive."

"Let's forget the past."

"Deal." Sealing it with a soft kiss, Gal felt the familiar firmness pressing against her. "He's baaack."

Lee tensed, his first thought leaping to her imaginary invader but then felt her hand on *his* party crasher. "Yes, and he's got a full tank."

"Perfect, I could go all night," she murmured. "Want to ditch this band stand?"

"Since I want to take you under the table right now, that's a hard yes. I have a room. Reserved it when I gave you the invite in case we drank too much, or just didn't feel like going home."

"I like your thinking, Cowboy." She frisked his tux, fishing out a pair of room keys, tucking one inside her bra.

"You know that situation I'm always in that you like ribbing me about?"

"Yes, this corundum conundrum? You're a diamond in the rough," she whispered, enjoying the challenge of touching him in public.

"Yeah, that. Just how I am supposed to leave the dance floor?"

"I'll stay close," she promised. She had a fleeting fantasy to tap him off right there in the middle of the ballroom without anyone the wiser. Maybe if she smashed herself against him, everyone would just think they were grinding. She made a bet with herself. If the next number was a slow one…

"Gal, be careful, you know I'm also an explosive kind of guy."

Chapter Seventeen

They could barely swipe the card, fumbling more with each other than the key. Lee didn't know how fortunate he was the band decided to take an intermission at that very moment, but just the idea of what she wanted to do was drenching enough.

Finally barging in, Gal flung off her heels and stripped Lee of his jacket, while he unzipped her dress and she yanked his loosened tie over his head. They fell on the bed in a lustful heap. Lee crawled on top, making her ovaries flutter with anticipation.

"Damn it. I left my handbag downstairs." She started to rise, hating to break the mood.

"They'll keep it at the front desk." His voice was deep and throaty as he ran his hand up her thigh, tempting her back on the pillow.

"I don't want it stolen. My credit card is in there."

"Cancel it," he mumbled, planting kisses down her neck.

"I won't feel relaxed until I have it. And while I'm out, I'll grab some ice." Nibbling his earlobe, her whisper lingered into a hiss, sweeping him into a sorcerer's spell. "I have a few tricks up my sleeve."

"That would be hot," he slurred, kissing her breasts elegantly held hostage by an ivory fleurs-de-lis print.

"I'll be back lickety-split."

"No, let me. It's the gentleman thing to do." But his lips refused to leave, neither of them going anywhere. "On the other hand," he said, bringing hers to his bulky trousers. "Where can I go with this?"

"Good point."

"Or, we can do it later. We have all night," he reminded, pulling her back on the bed.

It was tempting to wait, deterred by his delectable kisses, but if she didn't leave now, Gal knew she never would. She pushed him away gently.

"I don't want my gun getting into the wrong hands. I saw ice right down the hall. It'll be worth the wait, I swear."

"Hurry back," he begged, wrapping his arms around her from behind.

Managing to wriggle free, she snatched the bucket and bolted out the door. Her bare feet flounced across the tan carpet as she hurried to the lift near the dispenser. The illuminated numbers above the metal doors indicated the car was still many floors away. She tapped her foot impatiently, then deciding to save time, lined the cup under the spout and pulled the lever, watching cubes tumble out noisily, clanging and clinking. A foot away, the elevator dinged and as she ran to catch it, a man emerged carrying her clutch.

The bucket seemed to fall in slow motion, ice bouncing out in all directions but Galaxy froze, petrified.

"Hello, Galaxia." The man dressed in black with matching ascot and greasy ponytail menaced so close, his goatee scratched her cheek. Detecting the familiar stench of Yorsh, her stomach turned, but her heart felt nothing.

Still mixing Vodka with his Baltic Porter. "Viktor," she acknowledged coldly. "I thought I saw you earlier. I knew I wasn't crazy."

"Eh, I'm not so sure about that, hohol. Your mental state has always been a matter of question." He tossed her pocketbook at her feet.

"Why are you here?" she hissed, spittle spraying his face.

"Someone has to make sure you do your job."

"I'm keeping Lee out of the way, so you can do yours."

"Oh, I bet you are." He leered at her neckline now gaping because of the open zipper. "You were always good in the sack, weren't you, my little suka?" His tobacco-stained fingers stroked the curve of her face. "Your best skill was black bag jobs if I recall correctly." He chuckled at the crude innuendo, his rasp suggesting three packs a day.

"That's breaking and entering, you peshka!"

"My mistake. I suppose he's the one doing that, huh?" He copped a feel like he owned her. "Lucky bastard!"

How did she ever think she loved him? He was swine on the inside and out. She slapped his hand away, and he was shocked. "What exactly do you want?" Her crisp tone was eager to end the unpleasant exchange.

"This!" He plucked the keycard from her breasts, glancing at the sleeve. "Room two-fourteen. Good to know. Mine's in the purse."

A door squeaked open, and Lee appeared, robed. "Gal, what's taking so long?" Then, spotting her surrounded by spilled ice, he sprinted down the hall.

Viktor whispered something right before Gal bent down to scoop up the contents, then in slight-of-hand fashion, slipped into the elevator dispersing guests at just the right moment. She sighed relief when the doors swallowed him whole, not a second too soon.

Lee was at her side, immediately seizing the half-melted crescents and dumping them into the overflow grate. "Everything okay? What was that about?"

"Oh nothing, you know how clumsy I am. I was in such a rush to get back to you, I bumped into that guy. C'mon..." She led him away quickly, hoping he wouldn't ask any more questions.

Freshening up, her plan of playing it cool fell apart as soon as she closed the bathroom door. *Pull yourself together, girl.* She wasn't sure why she was crying. A mixed bag of her past, glad Lee hadn't caught on, betrayal, misgivings, finally getting over that scalawag once and for all.

Or was it the turmoil of new love and knowing it had to end? She plunged her face into cold water to blanch the emotions. She didn't want to spoil the evening, not when the only thing she was certain about was waiting on the other side of the door.

"I ordered champagne and refilled the ice

bucket," Lee announced, surprising her when she entered the room. Candles flickered, casting an attractive ambiance, accompanied by the soft romantic playlist humming from his phone. "You wanted a proper date."

The tears were back, brimming at his thoughtfulness. "It's beautiful. The whole evening's perfect."

"Are you sure you're okay? Something didn't seem right back there."

"Never better." She pushed him on the bed with an aggressive kiss, maybe more to convince herself than Lee.

He slipped off her gown inch by inch, grazing a trail of exposed skin along the way. When it gathered at her feet, she kicked off the remainder.

Insatiable by Darren Hayes harmonized their rendezvous so appropriately. The rising of the melodic notes teasing, building, craving, The hypnotic whisper of desire so powerful, it united their souls.

They went at each other hungrily; their bodies intertwined like twisted sheets, their love so visceral it reached the depths of their core. They collapsed, breathing one breath until a rapping on the door broke the euphoria.

Chapter Eighteen

The "Do Not Disturb" sign glared at them from the wrong side of the door. Lee cursed, realizing this oversight in their haste.

"It's maintenance. We have to swap out rotted trees."

The agents exchanged puzzled glances before shooting one at the room's fichus, which seemed fine, albeit a few dry, pitted leaves. "What the—" Lee mouthed silently.

"Sounds odd," Gal agreed, jumping up to grab a robe as Lee wrapped himself in his, packing heat.

"Be careful," she warned.

He peeked between the chain links. Two men in dingy, mustard uniforms manned a cart hosting a thriving tree.

"You're replacing plants at this hour?" Lee asked through the barrier.

"Just following orders, sir," one apologized.

"We're more likely to find patrons in the room this time of night," the other offered.

"Seems more appropriate to follow a maid during turnover," Lee advised. "Come back tomorrow when we've check out."

"Please, sir. Each pot has a room number on it. You'd be doing us a solid if you just take this off our hands. The faster we check them off, the faster we get home to our families."

Lee glanced at Gal behind the door. She nodded. "Okay, make it quick." He braced for action, just in case. Normally, he wouldn't have thought twice about this weird request, other than it being odd. He'd once stayed at a hotel on New Year's Eve where they delivered fresh towels at midnight because it became a funny tradition. A college football team requested them and won the Rose Bowl. But now with Galaxy's intuition about Viktor, he wasn't taking a chance.

The guys wheeled in the rubber tree and did a

quick swap, leaving with a nod.

"So, that seemed harmless and not suspicious at all," Gal giggled, replacing the chain.

"Hmm, what do you think that was about?" Reclining on the bed, he propped himself by an elbow.

Gal joined him, lying flat on her back. "It didn't look like anything was under the cart like I imagined."

"Were you expecting something?" he teased.

"No, just wishful thinking."

"My mind went there too. Maybe they were smuggling jewels."

"*Into* our room?" she chortled. "We should be so lucky."

A gnawing notion made him sit up. "Treasure hunt?"

They scrambled over and started digging. "Wait a minute. This isn't your way of proposing, is it?"

"Gee, Galaxy, don't be such a spoilsport," he scoffed in mock insult. "Yeah, right after a week of dating, I always go to the trouble of planting a diamond in a random tree and have it delivered with room service." They laughed at the absurdity.

"Actually, it's brilliant." They sifted through the soil for several minutes. "Sorry to disappoint you, but your theory is full of holes." She swiped mud on her robe.

"Unless..." he rose, pacing the room. "What if they were transporting something out? I can't shake the feeling that something was going on by the elevator. Be honest. It was him, wasn't it? Did he hurt you?" Kneeling beside her, he stroked her hair.

"I'm fine. He was just reminiscing about old times. The jerk misses me, I guess." She narrowed her eyes. "How did you know?"

"Why, because he didn't fit the description you gave me earlier? It doesn't take a cryptologist to read your body language. So why did you throw me off track?"

"I don't know. It was dumb. I was afraid I still had feelings for him, and I didn't want you there slanting the results. I never thought about being in actual danger."

"Fucking unbelievable!" Scrambling to his feet, he began blowing out candles. "Then what the hell are we doing here, Gal? Am I just some guy to screw until Viktor wakes up and smells the coffee?"

She sprang up, following him. "Wait, don't get mad! I just needed to test my heart, to make sure."

"And did it pass?" he glared, shoving legs into boxer shorts.

"Aced it!"

"Meaning..."

"Meaning, I'm over him! Forever. Caput. His groping and nasty insults confirmed it."

"And that's the kind of guy you like?"

"Definitely not. I don't know what I was thinking. Blinded by youth, I guess. I joined Firebird as if I could help change the world." She huffed at such a farce. "To think I let him mold me. He's not even worth all the calories I scarfed down." She slid down the edge of the bed onto the carpet. "Why do women do that? It's stupid. I bet men don't drown themselves in self-pity."

"Why do you think beer was invented?" He hugged a pillow, flopping down on the floor. "So does that mean we can finally put him out to pasture? Because, frankly, my dear, I am quite sick of that guy."

"That makes two of us." She inched closer and put her hand on his. "Our evening tonight sealed the deal. I knew... it's you!"

He pulled her into his arms, still a bit guarded. "Glad to hear that, but seriously, you said if he was hanging around, it was bad news. What's he up to?"

"He... just wanted me back is all." She got up, pouring another round of drinks.

Lee studied her. "We should keep an eye out just in case. Maybe we should check around again."

"We should be careful, yes. But for tonight, everything's fine. I told him loud and clear, I wasn't interested."

"Good." They sat against the bed, listening to

the soothing music, half asleep from the booze. "Wait, there's just something that keeps bugging me. How did he know where to find you?"

"Oh…he said he'd been watching me all night, jealous," she shivered. "No wonder I sensed it! He saw us go into the hotel, dressed to the nines. And then when we left, he stalked us to the second floor."

"Well, that's creepy. I wonder why we didn't cross paths, or where he started from."

"Excellent question. He's a pro at hiding. Oh great, now I'm starting to freak out!" She rubbed imaginary chills on her arms.

"Didn't mean to scare you. I was just thinking out loud. We'll call for backup security on our way home. No worries." He caressed her back then pointed to the pot. "Guess it was just Arbor Day after all. Let's hit the sack."

"Yeah, if I can sleep now. Thanks."

"Who said anything about sleep?"

They got up to stand, her terrycloth pocket accidentally snagging a long strand of bamboo, which promptly unzipped the planter. "Oops." She held up the ripped evidence in embarrassment.

"Congratulations," he chuckled. "You ruined something that's been here for about five minutes."

"Maybe management won't notice," she offered, chewing a hangnail.

Lee bent over to investigate. "Only minor damage," he reported, braiding it back on.

"Let me guess; you took basket weaving in high school?"

He looked up. "No, for a case on a commune."

"Of course." It was Gal's turn to shake her head.

Just then a frayed edge rolled apart between his fingers. "Hey, this peels away. Look!" They knelt down and removed the inner cane layer. Something flat covered in plastic wrapped around the circumference of the pot. They wriggled it free.

"Well, I'll be..." Gal dashed to the door and surveyed the hall.

"Amazing! How'd they think to fit a painting in here? What are you doing?" he asked, noticing her nervous energy.

"Checking for lurking suspects but the coast looks clear."

"We better not unroll the canvas. Don't want to risk damaging it, might be famous. Doesn't it look familiar?"

"Yes, where do you think it's from?" Gal looked closely at the folded face of a sad little redhead peeking around the creased canvas, a salmon-pink bow in her hair. She was almost lost in an oversized white dress sitting there in the grainy wooden chair. Gal rotated the package, looking for an identifying marker. "I think it says *Ruth*, or Rutherford something, maybe? I'm not sure. It bends."

"Artist or subject? Could be from any museum around here." Lee pulled out his phone. "Do you think all the replacements have one or this just happened to be a lucky drop? Seems a little too convenient if you ask me, especially with Viktor lurking around."

"Why would he send us a stolen painting? He'd

want it far away from us as possible. Are you reporting this or taking a picture?"

"I'm calling Geoff."

"At this hour?"

"Right, I should call the police."

"Not yet. Let's check on other trees first. Get a better handle on whether it's a major operation or single incident." Gal jumped into her gown, slipping on her heels.

"At this hour? What do we do, knock on doors?"

"Good thinking. It's nearly midnight; we can't do that." She looked around, flailing for an idea. "We could split up, look around the hotel, see if any hallway or lobby displays have a secret prize inside."

"Or, we could call this in, give the authorities the lead." His thumb flew across the keypad. Gal covered his hand, lowering it.

"What fun is that? Don't you want to see where this goes?"

"Sure, but—"

"Are we investigators or not? Would you rather

have a confident story to tell Geoffrey or do you want to tick him off again?"

Lee sighed, knowing she was right. It was important to collect facts. "I think we better act fast if we have any hope of trailing deliveries." Tossing his phone on the bed, he resumed dressing, lining his pockets with essentials.

"I have the room key," Gal announced, tucking it into her pleats along with her diminutive handgun. "I wish I packed a change of clothes." She curtsied in exasperated sarcasm.

"You win Best Dressed agent hands down," he joked, kissing her forehead.

"Thanks. Oh, what am I thinking? I can run better barefoot." She flung off her footwear.

"Oh good, you mean those aren't weapons?"

"Not yet," she smiled. They scampered down the hall, taking the stairwell three steps at a time. From the lobby, they had a clear view of the glass encased tiers. Minimal movement peppered throughout the floors that time of night as only a few sleepy guests meandered the halls returning from the dance or nearby tourist attractions.

"This reminds me of the ant farm I had as a kid," Lee remarked.

Those little traitors..."Lucky! I always asked for one, but Father Christmas never came through. I dreamt of being the queen of the colony."

"Ah, the gateway to world domination." He feigned an evil laugh. "Well, they were pretty cool until I forgot to feed them and they all died, along with my dream of becoming an Entomologist. Of course, most of the bunch were DOA anyway." Appraising the atrium, he signaled toward a hiding spot near a potted tree. "Let's hope we don't get the same result tonight."

"I'm sorry your bug dreams were squashed. I guess you traded them for the electronic kind."

"Thanks," Lee smiled, his glance lingering while Gal ripped open the planter.

She came up empty. "Maybe they're just in the rooms?"

The desk clerk frowned and headed their way but was stopped by a pajamaed patron. They ducked inside a back door, scurrying out of sight just in time.

"We should check a few more before coming to that deduction, but we can't keep destroying their property. We better move fast, c'mon." He led them up a stairway.

"I think we should divide and conquer. We'll cover more ground."

Lee gave her a doubtful look. "Yeah, like when I was fake searching Viktor?"

"I said I was sorry. It didn't think that through."

"I know, but this time I'm not taking any chances."

"Seriously, I mean it. If we want to intercept those maintenance men, it's our best bet."

After careful thought, he relented. "No funny business. It's only to increase our odds."

"I promise! I'll go left. You take a right." To prove her alliance, she initiated a deep kiss.

"I'll go left. You go right," he said, not letting her

call the shots.

She watched Lee sprint off and sighed relief. Chalk one up for reverse psychology! She raced to a room on the third floor finding the door ajar and Viktor taking a painting off the wall.

"So, you call this a lair?" Leaning lazily against the doorway, her words startled him. Vik dropped the frame, shattering glass.

"A good a place as any. It has room service."

Gal spied a partial slab of steak on a table behind him. "Yeah, better than that underground bunker in Kungurskaya." A wistfulness infused her voice. They had been on the run, the danger and excitement exhilarating, and she had lost herself in him. "So when did this turn into *Masterpiece Theatre?* We're supposed to release Legionella into the White House, not rip-off Rembrandts. By the way, aren't paintings supposed to breathe?"

"What are you now, a curator? Besides, I never gave a boar's ball about Ukraine. This is more lucrative."

"I suppose Kat is calling the shots now?"

"You know what a cat burglar she is," he cackled. He bent down to pick off the shards. "So did you ditch the lunk and finally come to your senses?" Harvesting gristle from his teeth with a glass splinter, her repulsion returned. It was then she realized her real enemy was nostalgia.

"I told you before. I want out. Permanently this time!"

"I knew you were too soft for this. Always were." He slipped Martha Washington out of the cheap frame and chuckled, "The closest thing you are to being an assassin is that nice ass."

"You're disgusting, Vik. Have you always been this crass or is your lifestyle catching up to you?"

"Humph, I'm the same. You are the one who changed. Too in love with that imbecile. It's made you weak."

"I just stopped him from calling in that stolen painting. No easy task."

"Child's play. If you want to prove yourself,

shoot him!"

"That's a bit drastic," she faltered, their exchange quickly turning into a game of truth or dare.

"Ha, just as I thought."

Gal whipped her pistol from her breasts, pressing it to his head. "Do you know how many times I've pictured *your* brains splattered like a Jackson Pollock?"

Viktor laughed. "You don't have it in you. Could tell when we trained. You're a nurse, not a kill—"

The gun cocked.

He swiftly stuck his silencer into her stomach. "We end this now, or you get out of here—Go!"

Stumbling from the room in tears, she rounded the corner to the elevator, heart pounding. If he hadn't counter-offered, would she have had the guts to oft him?

Still shaken and a bit out of breath, she caught up with Lee in a nearby stairwell. "Any luck?"

"Nope, nothing. I checked another planter,

turned up empty. How about you?" He studied her carefully. Something or more accurately *someone* had her rattled.

Gal could tell he was onto her. Maybe he could see the adrenaline pumping through her veins. "Nada. I had to flag down a delivery man, and he was confrontational, that's all. I managed to sweet-talk my way into getting a peek, but it was just a swap." She traipsed behind him a few flights, serenity returning. "Well, this feels familiar."

"What? You've chased after flower pots before?" he asked, amused.

"No," she laughed. "The basement tunnels, the musty spiral steps. Glad this one has plenty of fresh air."

"Oh right! That night seems like a million years ago, doesn't it?" They stopped at a landing overlooking the lobby. "That's it, Gal! The White House. The painting was outside Anita's office."

"Oh yeah," she remembered, a vague illustration forming in her mind. "But there must be more than one painting of that girl, right?"

"Maybe, although I think most art there is one of a kind. How do you suppose they got it out without anyone noticing?"

"Hmm, I don't know. With all that security, it had to be professional."

"My thoughts exactly. Could only mean one thing— your Kat."

"Yes, but she's not my Kat. She's yours…and, you know who."

"Right! And like fools, we left the painting unattended! I bet that's the whole ruse; it's a pickup!" Panic flew him down flights of stairs, racing him to the room. They burst inside.

Everything looked fine until he spied the wicker vessel tipped over, dirt clumps spilling on the rosebud carpet. He paced, running his hands through his hair in despair.

He spun around, angrily pinning her to the wall, so close their noses touched. "You!" For a split second, he wanted to kiss her. "You've been in on it all along! I should've followed my gut. You kept me from turning over evidence, and like an idiot, I let you. Geoff will have my head. I could be fired. No, I should be!"

"Calm down, James Bond, and thanks for the vote of confidence. I knocked the planter over when I tossed my shoes. And I put the painting in the safe for good measure."

He loosened the grip on her shoulder and backed away, ashamed.

She walked over, pulled the canvas from its hiding place, and threw it on the bed. "Paranoid much?"

Picking up the parcel, he apologized. "Now Viktor's presence is weirding *me* out."

"Yeah, welcome to my world."

"We better lock this up and report it. Wait a minute..." Flipping the package over in his hands, he made a startling discovery. "This isn't the same painting!"

Chapter Nineteen

In the murky realm of watercolors running like melting clocks, Lee unwrapped the mock masterpiece. "It's not even close. The exaggerated bow and wrong shade of pink gives it away, not to mention the primitive smiley face. And this is much smaller, fits easily in the safe. The original was much too big. In fact, the whole painting is off, like an abstract Picasso or...a bad dream." He held it out, expecting an explanation.

"That's weird. I honestly put it in the safe. It did fit," she mumbled.

"You did no such thing, did you? We left it on the bed. You never touched it."

"You got me," she conceded with no place to go, aiming her handgun at him. "I'm sorry to spoil our romantic evening. It really was perfect!" A tear slid down her cheek.

"So you've been on his side the whole time," Lee challenged, gun out, heart ripped to shreds.

"Vik took my key at the ice machine. Shortly before we left the ballroom, a text arrived from his team saying our room would be the dead drop for the smuggled paintings, demanding to know what floor. I was to perform my part from there. It would have been a piece of cake if I hadn't ripped the planter."

"So it was no accident you were by the elevator. You were so determined to get your purse. I knew something seemed off. Wait—you said you didn't find him earlier, but you failed to mention he contacted you! Never mind, why do I believe anything when you sent me on a snipe hunt? How many paintings are there? Are they in every guest room?"

"I only know of three. The most valuable ones, less noticeable that way. And yes, when I thought I saw him at the end of our dance, I went looking but didn't find him. I didn't even know he was in town.

Honest! He rarely gets his hands dirty these days. But when we split up, his men started harassing me with texts, insisting I give them information I didn't have. I didn't know we had a room until just before we left, and that's when I did the only thing I had time to do without you noticing—quickly text '2' behind my back. I was instructed earlier to leave my bag."

"He still had your cell number? You said there weren't any tracers."

"No, I…I had my number changed, but he must have swapped my phone, which is why I caught a glimpse of him. Yes, I gave you a bogus lead. I couldn't let you follow me, and I couldn't tell you about the message."

"Yeah, yeah, you told me, you wanted to see if you still had feelings for the scoundrel. Blah, blah, blah. Well boohoo, Gal and surprise! I saw your secret Soviet phone in your special drawer. I bugged it. And downstairs, I followed you instead of splitting up. You were texting someone. You seemed agitated then and later at the ice machine. I knew it had to be the infamous V because again, you were upset."

"Great, so you broke into my desk! I guess that makes us even. What great partners we are, huh?" A hybrid sound bubbled up her throat, and she wasn't sure whether to laugh or cry. "But wiring was a waste of time because he only sends texts, self-destructing ones at that. We hadn't spoken in over a year."

"Until tonight's gabfest that is. Yeah, that's right, the bug is also a tracking device. I followed you to his room too."

"Then you heard me quit."

"Personally, I was rooting for you to pull the trigger."

"Please understand how complicated this all is. I hate lying to you, but I was forced to keep you away. Viktor threatened to kill my father if you tagged along." She gulped back tears. Had it come down to this, bullying each other with bullets?

"Why would Viktor murder your father if *I* showed up? Talk about overkill."

Anguish contorted her pretty face. "Because he would know then that I traded sides. His organization has my dad hostage, along with several teams from DWB. I had no choice. But when Vik stepped off the elevator tonight, I knew I wanted out completely. Somehow I had to break his chains of leverage, even if it cost me everything."

"Ah, the bleeding heart move. Well played as usual, but I don't believe anything you say anymore."

"Believe me then." Viktor barged in, brash and repugnant. He threw the original package on top of the tangled bedding, then added the latest canvas, folded and tucked into a Sunday edition of the *Washington Post*. "You like the new painting?" he crowed, pointing to the replacement.

Lee's face squared, not amused.

"My five-year-old drew it," he chortled, entertained by his own cleverness. "Or should I say *our* darling daughter?" He stroked Gal's hair as she flinched.

Well! If this new information was true, it

definitely explained a few things. But if Viktor was expecting a gaping mouth reaction, Lee refused to give him the satisfaction. "Then why are you holding her grandfather hostage?"

"They're not that close." Viktor motioned his weapon at Lee and the closet. "You can hang around while we gather our effects."

"I'm not going anywhere," Lee stated. "But you are."

That gave Viktor a gruff belly laugh. He turned to Gal. "With everything great you say about him, I guess he's no mathematician."

Manhandling Lee by the arm, he shoved him toward the empty clothes rack, but Lee's muscular build stood tall, overshadowing him. Vik's voice escalated in anger. "Get in there so we can call it a night!" He squeezed Gal's caboose and snickered, "We have some catching up to do."

Lee noticed Gal about to vomit. Maybe she was telling the truth. On the other hand, she did have a lot of champagne. He caught her eye and nodded, not even sure they were on the same page.

While Viktor's womanizing pupils drooled down her cleavage, Gal drove a bullet deep into his hand, causing him to drop the firearm. Vik howled, stunned, the sting severe at close range.

Lee lunged for it, quickly becoming a two-fisted bandit. "Hey, I was supposed to do that," he complained, beaming with admiration.

"Well, now you won't have to." Head held high, she tried concealing a smile.

"Where are the paintings? How did they get out of the White House?"

Viktor, even while cornered, didn't back down. "Ha, you want a brainy back story. But no do. I don't rat my team." They watched as he unbuttoned his shirt with his good hand, bracing themselves for a retaliating arsenal. But instead, sliding it off and utilizing grungy teeth, he tore a strip of cloth to wrap around his mitt.

"Surely, this is the work of a grand art thief. Nothing you can pull off, Vik," Lee baited. "Where's your wife, the great Katjarina? I'd love to say hello for old time's sake."

"*She* is my wife!" he barked, a sharp nod toward Gal.

Lee's left eyebrow shot up in surprise, never having considered this possibility. His head was spinning. Of course, he would know she was not the same woman unless she was also a master shapeshifter.

"You're a delusional two-timer, Viktor," she spat back. "You called off our engagement for Kat."

"Don't lie in front of your boyfriend, Galaxia." He looked at Lee. "She *is* Katja! Pull off the wig and see."

"Lee, no, he's a pathological liar," she sputtered, holding onto her tresses.

He tensed, the vein in his neck throbbing. The surreal scene wasn't adding up. But suddenly Andle's words made complete sense. *One of the samples is synthetic.* He took a step toward Gal, then stopped.

"You know what, it doesn't matter. I don't care

who's hitched to whom or whose hand rocked the cradle. This is an international crime, not the *Jerry Springer* show."

"Come on, Lee, we both know what he said isn't true."

"Whatever, Gal. As long as the cows are in the barn at sunset, it's all the same day's work." Their eyes met painfully. This wasn't how the evening was supposed to end. "All I care about are the artifacts. Where are they?"

Viktor smirked, pleased to unnerve the dynamic duo. "It's not that easy, lover boy. She doesn't know, and I won't tell."

"Viktor, the van is loaded and waiting—oh boy!" A wiry man burst into the room, nearly knocking Gal off her feet. He skidded to a halt when he saw the agent pointing two guns at his grumpy boss.

"Fitzy?" Lee and Gal asked in unison.

"If you call jinx, the next person who speaks owes you a soda."

"You're in on this?" Lee, dumbfounded, ignored his suggestion.

"I'm the master thief," he said in grandeur, his chest inflating along with his ego.

Laughter escaped the agents, including Viktor despite his discomfort. None of them could picture this wimp the wizard behind the curtain. Could it be the least suspected suspect was under their nose the whole time?

"You don't b-believe me!" he scowled, cheeks flaring. "It-it was the perfect s-set up. I distract the White House, throw a t-tantrum, and demand my rights. Every t-time I met with Anita, I was casing the place, on the look-out for the best art, the ones easily replaced without t-tipping a red f-flag."

"Clever," Lee kudo'ed. "But what was replacing them? Certainly not these preschool scribbles?"

"Counterfeit copies, one at a time. Once we popped a painting from the frame, we stashed them inside tree planters hanging in plain sight as hotel art. We stockpiled all week until breaking them out for the get-away." Fitz paced importantly, pointing out their genius plan.

"How many?" Lee asked, wanting a number once and for all, knowing Fitz was the guy to give it.

"Seven. One each day," he boasted.

"And Tom helped you sneak around," Galaxy guessed, remembering the bugged calls.

"He was the only one to believe my story. And when no one would help me, I convinced him to let me take valuable artwork for compensation."

"No, Tom showed *me* around. *I'm* the master thief!" The clicking of fingernails on the doorjamb got their attention as a vivacious woman entered. "Looks like you forgot to invite me to the party." She appraised the room, pouring herself a flute of bubbly. "Not nice taking credit for my career, Gerald. After all, I don't go around claiming to be a dog walker."

He looked like his deflated self again. The women exchanged looks of disdain.

Lee scrutinized her face. "But you *do* go around pretending to be my girlfriend and a librarian, don't you, Kate?"

Addressing him in puppy speak, a sad reminiscent smile turned her pouty lips as she caressed his chest. "Ah, Clancy. Did you miss me? No, never an old spinster librarian, not me," she purred, showcasing her figure in a gold leopard print dress, flipping her platinum bob. "But an intern, yes, at the L.O.C. That's where I met Gerry's mother, Johanna. She knew where to find the architectural blueprints, so we schemed up the lost Kennedy." She crowed at their cunningness. Then she stopped laughing and shot an infuriated scowl at Fitz. "She was always yakking my ear off about the Kennedys like they were Tsars or something. If you ask me, they were just a bunch of privileged khuligans."

So Kat *was* Kate! Gal had only guessed before. Connecting the dots seemed likely, and she enjoyed giving Lee a hard time about it, not really believing it until now. She had a sinking feeling she couldn't shake—sympathy for Lee, jealousy perhaps? Definitely annoyance at this apparition always plaguing her side.

"At first, the idea was supposed to be believable, keeping them busy looking into it. But they refused me from the start, and I got mad, so that seemed to work better." Fitz was a chatterbox, gloating like a child staying up past his bedtime.

"Why would his mother get involved and risk her job?" Lee asked Kat. He realized he was still aiming the handguns at Viktor, but only Galaxy was pointing anything at him.

"Sour grapes, I guess," Kat sneered. "Not my problem. We need to get a move on, chop, chop!" She clapped her hands to corral the others, creeping toward the door.

"Just a minute, Katja. I have some questions." Gal stepped over, blocking the way.

"I'll give you one. Go." She folded her arms, flaunting clout with her upturned nose.

"If you're so desirable, why did you need to rely on a love potion to seduce Lee, huh? Why hide pheromones in his toilet tank?"

"I did no such thing, and that was two questions." She bustled forward.

Gal cast a surprising shrug at Lee. "Then how did a vial of Bombykol get there?"

"Look at me, darling. Do I need pheromones? Now if you excuse me, little suka, I have places to be." She pushed past Galaxy's folded arms, but Gal stood her ground, tired of being called a bitch by these self-important lowlifes. Remembering who she was, she threw her weight forward, knocking Kat back.

"Our lab tech said it was moth pheromones," Gal blared, feeling defiant, and now foolish hearing it out loud.

"Do you believe everything your lab man tells you?"

Her snickering indicated an inside joke she was not privy to. Suddenly she was back in grade school, slurping a thermos of borsch and crunchy smelt while derogatory half-breed names taunted her in Irish dialect. She hadn't known the meaning, but the negative tone stung like stones. Now Gal lobbed a look at Lee, imploring him to toss her a lifeline after defending him in that small way.

Lee surveilled the scene like a sweeping light beacon. "The vial's mine," he admitted, at last.

"After all your denials, you used it…" Punched in the gut by betrayal, Gal could barely breathe.

"No, they aren't chemicals of attraction," he assured her. "It's spy dust."

"So you dusted me with this stuff?"

"No, I never put anything on you. It's not even pheromone. It's illumination powder. What we have is pure, unadulterated heat."

Kat retched in protest. "Silly girl, what good would it do to hide a vial labeled correctly? That would be too obvious."

"So, you're working with them! You're still with *her* then." The slap of infidelity chafed her cheek, the words thorns on her tongue. She clasped the doorknob to steady herself.

"Not a chance. I'm rogue."

"Why you double crosser—" Kat menaced.

Lee continued to aim the revolvers at the riffraff. "But we were an item last year when, unbeknownst to me, the heist was hatched. Once I caught on, I only pretended to help, and we broke up soon after. I didn't know she was the great Katjarina. So tell me, Kate, why the hook-up if you were married to *him*?" It was obvious Galaxy's heart wasn't the only one pilfered by these two.

Defying the threshold, Katja stepped close, whispering into his ear. "You've heard of keeping your friends close and your enemy right under your nose." She traced his lips with a perfect manicured finger. He had the urge to bite it, to chomp it clean off.

"I know that one well," he acknowledged, eyeing Gal. "So why did Viktor sever ties instead of keeping *her* under his wing?" He gestured with the gun, determined not to let Katjarina get to him.

"Who says he hasn't?" Kat scowled at her husband.

"These are much more questions than just one," Viktor grouched.

The thieves edged past the doorway, barely crossing into the hall. Lee shot Kat and Vik in the foot simultaneously, while Gal fired at Fitzy, disabling the getaway.

"Do I need to shoot you too?" he asked, still mistrustful of her motives.

She shook her head, admiring his gun-slinging. "Not unless I shoot you first." And they were back where they were before the interruptions.

"Do it Galaxia, don't be a fool," Vik commanded, writhing in pain.

Just for the hell of it, relying on the reflection from the dresser mirror, she pinged a bullet over her shoulder, right into the left arm of her ex-fiancé instead.

"Cool," Lee nodded, captivated by her callous skill.

Vik yelped, and Kat smacked him, making him wince thrice.

"Don't think I'm happy about your little reunion," she hissed.

"I can say the same," he grumbled.

"I guess this means we're not hopping that flight to Paris?" Fitz wailed.

Chapter Twenty

"The traveling art show is over, Kreskinovas!" Audra appeared, armed with arresting agents, who didn't waste time cuffing all three. "Who's this guy?"

"Fitzy Baker, if that's his real name." Lee flashed his handgun in the form of a question.

"Coopersmith, Fitzgerald Coopersmith," he whimpered, nursing his ankle. "Can I get a Band-Aid?" he whined, limping away.

"Smitty!" Gal guessed.

"Galaxy, my sweet gal!" Audra drawled then tsked, clinking handcuffs on her friend. "I never thought I'd have to turn you in. Then again, I never thought I'd be weeding your apartment for evidence either." She took a matchbook out of her pocket and handed it to Lee.

"That's it?" Baffled, he flipped through a tiny blank notebook.

"Invisible ink," Audra explained, tossing an ultraviolet pen his way. "Details of their intimidation tactics, forcing the president to increase troops in Crimea."

Lee clicked on the light, hovering over the pages as the plan materialized, shaking his head. "Biological warfare? Pretty harsh way to save your country."

"Just a hypothetical backup," Galaxy defended, dazed at the ambush. "We knew we'd never have to use it."

Audra flashed the KGB badge, handing it back to her. "Deactivated six years ago."

Gal tucked it into her bra, looking from Lee to Audra betwixt bewildered sputterings of, "You searched my place?" and, "I thought you quit."

"No," Audra chuckled. "When Kate had her hissy fit, it looked like a good time to ghost behind the scenes. I dug into research, where we met. We knew something was up when a painting disappeared from the Smithsonian during that time.

We didn't realize Kate was Katjarina until recently. Good work on the hair sample."

"We?" she asked, drained. Sides were changing faster than a ping pong game.

"I didn't just stumble upon that George Washington painting. I knew it had been tampered with, so I was checking its condition, making sure the camera bug was still intact. Like Andle said, it's much too big to waltz out with. The joke's on them, though; it's just an artist's copy, purposely embedded with a typo on one of George's books. The secret passage was a surprise, though."

"Secret passage?" Audra noticed their matching blushes.

"Never mind," Lee chuckled.

Audra led Galaxy away, following the bunch toward the elevator, eventually leading to unmarked cars.

"Go easy on her, huh?" Lee called down the hall. He looked around the room, feeling a bit vitriolic. Lying back on the bed, he sighed, restless. Another wasted segment of life bound and gagged by emotion. He knew better than to fall for her but it was as autonomic as breathing, which at the moment was hard to do with a heavy chest and tight throat.

Galaxy wasn't wrong about the evening being perfect, and no matter how it ended, it had been worth it. No, scratch that. If he was being honest— and let's face it, selfish—he preferred a different outcome; one that involved an entire night of pillow talk and making googly eyes at breakfast. Well, no use staying over now. It was too painful. He gathered his things, tucking the bulky newspaper under his arm as he shuffled down the humid stairwell. Nothing would ever be the same again.

The lobby was tranquil late at night, the quiet click of the keyboard a contrast to the precarious conflict moments ago. Rotating through the revolving door, a sudden curiosity spun like a lariat.

Whistling the tune *Insatiable,* he ducked around the corner to the ground level parking garage. Yes, the waiting van was still there, puffs of exhaust smogging up the concrete enclosure. Unbelievable, no one thought to intercept the vehicle holding the rest of the paintings? It was the perfect escape.

He approached with caution, sliding in shotgun and poising his pistol at the driver. "The jig is up!"

"That's always been your problem, Cowboy," Gal quipped, flooring the gas as soon as he slammed the door.

"You noticed that too?" Audra chirped from the back.

"What? You two were in cahoots?" Lee's heart soared.

"We thought it up lingerie shopping," Gal winked.

"We always wondered what would happen if agents got away with the goods for once. We were just pipe dreaming, though," Audra tittered.

"Without the pipe," Gal teased.

"And then you saw the opportunity," he speculated, incorporating his own involvement. When he tossed the bundle into Audra's lap, a vial fell from his pocket, bouncing onto the console.

"What's that?" Gal asked.

"Nothing." Lee tried jamming it back in, but Audra snatched it.

"Pheromones, that's what," she accused. "Did you get this from Lainey?"

"No, don't worry, it's a fake label. It's spy dust." Gal felt a bit superior, having been there for the unveiling.

"Naw, it's Bombykol," he admitted, exhausted from all the charades.

"What? So, it *is* a real substance then? I feel like it's been this phantom thing between us." It was more than she could digest, so she pulled the van into an empty Starbucks lot.

"You betcha it's real. But Andle's right. It doesn't work on humans, and I didn't use it on you. Just the paintings."

"So you were claiming them for yourself?" Gal asked in shock.

"Not exactly. I dabbed a few with glow powder

to mark it, as well as the infamous moth bait. Lainey
works at the Museum of Natural History in the insect
department. She had better success with her ant farm
than I did."

Galaxy couldn't believe the turn of events. *Just
when you think you know the man you love.* "So you
wanted to lure moths and ruin valuable paintings?"
She put the van in drive, speeding off.

"No, quite the contrary. I was protecting them.
The female pheromones attract the males, and in
turn, the substance sticks to them. The whole thing
becomes a masquerade ball, causing confusion as the
males hit on each other, making fools of themselves.
It's all very Shakespearean."

"Or Freudian," Audra slipped in.

"My plan was to protect the paintings but also
let Tom know which ones to guard. He knew any
marked art was about to be lifted."

"You were working with Tom all along? But he
led them right to it. Fitzy said he showed him
around, Kat too." Gal got on I-95, heading toward

Baltimore, more confused than ever.

"Yep, we paved a fool's paradise. Or in our case, a three idiots' Utopia. Lainey told me which paintings were the most valuable. By the way, she's Smitty."

"Ohhh, clever."

"So when I paid my first visit planting my original bug, the one I said I heard Urdu? I was pre-tagging the valuables."

"Yeah, I wondered what became of your Pakistani theory. It seemed to evaporate overnight."

"So are we still turning these in, or keeping them for ourselves now?" Audra asked, taking the additional canvases out of the newspaper.

"Chuck 'em."

Galaxy nearly hit a Jersey barrier. "Are you nuts? They must be priceless!"

"Yeah, if we sell them we can retire in style," Audra protested.

"You're right, Gal, about the *less* part. Tom deterred Kat, tricking her into taking reproductions created by local art students."

That brought a round of hysterics. The pretentious pair weren't any smarter than common criminals.

"So, we're still the good guys!" Audra smiled at the irony.

"I'm afraid so."

Galaxy grinned, pleased. For the first time in days, relief relaxed her. Finally free from the shackles of her past, she didn't want to be bound again.

"We can give the portraits back to the artists. Of course, there's one you might like to keep," he hinted, holding his hand out to Audra, who passed him the stack. Just then, the roving beam of a highway lamp fell on a headline. She snatched *The Post* back as Lee grabbed the inner contents.

"Whoa, guys! Get a load of this: *'Kennedy Heir Revealed! DNA testing proved Fitzgerald Coopersmith, 54, of Kennedy Kennels and Dog Walking, the grandson of President John F. Kennedy. Coopersmith is the son of JFK's love child from his teens, Jareth F. Kennedy and Johanna Franco Coopersmith, an intern at the White*

House during the Kennedy administration.' "

"Well, I'll be. It looks like his claim was partly right. Gal, so you did get his DNA sample after all?" Lee asked.

"No, we never had time, except the day he blew us off. Audra, did you?"

"No, I wasn't on the beat." She scanned the words. "Ah, looks like Mamie got it done. *'Joanna took charge when the current administration refused acknowledgment and had her son re-tested for confirmation.'* Hmm, interesting, Kennedy's people pinned paternity on JFK, assuming Johanna had relations with John, so they bribed her with a hush fund. Apparently, the First Lady was suspicious of all interns, so they hurried Johanna out, not listening nor bothering to check. And long before that happened, she wasn't taken seriously on the job, even though she had a library degree with a minor in art history. So there's your motive."

"Sour grapes? I'd say balsamic vinegar," Lee interjected. When the women looked at him funny, he came clean. "I went undercover as a chef once."

"I knew it!" Gal whispered, giving the steering wheel a victorious slap.

"But why, after all this time, would Johanna come forward? Must be something more valuable than coinciding with an art robbery," Lee wondered.

"Always the cynic," Audra sighed, skimming the rest of the story. "Oh no, she has cancer, the poor lamb. Stage four. She wanted to make sure Fitz got his due before she passed. Now that's a mama bear for you."

"That's so sweet," Gal gasped. Not so much in surprise, but to keep from crying, the effect of the evening getting the best of her.

"Speaking of mama bears…" Lee touched her elbow. "Is that a fact or a game of Viktor gone mad?"

"Oh!" It was a question she never expected to answer, although, after the night of tilt-o-whirl confessions, she should have seen it coming. "Um, unfortunately, it is. I mean, yes, it's true."

"Unfortunately? No need to apologize. I'm just

stunned it never came up."

"We are spies, you moron." Audra slapped his arm in solidarity. "We have to protect our families."

"Thank you," Gal called, smiling into the rearview mirror.

Had she known all along? Lee figured as much since girls dished secrets and gathered like geese in bathrooms. And apparently, modeled intimate apparel for each other.

"Oh, she mentioned her family," he said to Audra. "Even Viktor came up, but this little tidbit slipped her mind."

"Of course, I don't mean unfortunately, since I love Anya to pieces, but would you want to broadcast breeding with him? It was accidental, caught up in passion, adventure, and what I thought was love. Speaking of little tidbits, to be honest, when you first took me to Lainey's, I thought Travis was yours."

"What?" Lee laughed at such an outrageous idea. "Nope, Tray's my nephew, nothing more. Hey, they're about the same age. We should arrange a playdate."

"By Skype?" she chuckled, then sighed. "It breaks my heart to be so far away, and I'm lucky my folks are helping me out. She couldn't be raised by anyone better." The tears from her lashes stung, magnifying the glare on the road.

"Does Viktor's organization really have hostages?" he asked, remembering her father.

"Not for long," Audra's southern drawl interrupted. "I made the call before we arrested them. The FBI contacted Interpol, and they're on a rescue mission as we speak."

Gal let out a whoop, relieved for the second time that day. "Audra, I owe you a caviar farm! But how did you know?"

"I've been hovering like a honey bee and overheard your conversation earlier." She noticed their shock turn to awkward discomfort. "What? I told you I went into the shadows."

"But, you didn't *see* anything, right?" Lee

squirmed, replaying their romantic rendezvous.

"Don't worry; I know when to tune out. And Lee's not the only electronic bug planter. And I do mean *plant*."

"The trees!" Gal epiphanied.

"Yes. While lurking around the libe, I got wind of their plot, so I lodged a device into the weave of the basket lined up on your room cart in the maintenance room."

"Sharp thinking, Aud! We never even noticed. You're so good at stealth mode, are you going to stay in the background or come join us front and center?"

"You can take my place again," Galaxy offered.

"Gal, no! We are so great together." His voice cracked, disappointment welling up in his throat. He hadn't meant to be transparent, but he supposed there was no point in hiding his feelings now. There was so much more he wanted to say, but not here.

"Thanks, I think so too, but I decided earlier tonight, I'm going home. I miss my baby girl. When I told Vik I wanted out, I meant for good, the whole works. I should probably be on my own for a while, just Anya and me. I'll go back into nursing. It's safer. I mean that for you, too," she winked.

"Yeah, the week's been a wild ride," he sighed, rubbing the back of his arm. They rode in sad silence for several miles until something occurred to him. "Hey, the case is officially closed. I promised you a hammock on a beach if I recall."

"Hmm, I could go lackadaisical," Gal agreed. "There's plenty of romantic spots in Ireland. Everyone in?"

"It's tempting, but I'm sure you don't want a tricycle when you're pedaling a tandem."

A tollbooth loomed ahead. "Anyone have any change? Audra, are you sure? It feels rude to exclude you."

"Don't worry about me. I'm going to laze on a beach and down enough umbrella drinks to create my own shade," she assured, digging single bills from her pocket while Lee checked the glovebox for an E-Z Pass.

"That does sound heavenly."

"Not as much as Paris!" Lee produced three plane tickets and fake passports instead. "Looks like they were hitting the Louvre next. Flight leaves tonight on Aer Lingus, with an *Irish layover,*" he announced, tantalizing Gal with the tickets.

"In Dublin?" Galaxy guessed. "Oh no! They weren't going to Paris at all!" She slowed the van to pay, eclipsed by the emotional toll.

"What makes you think that?" Lee asked

"It's his pattern. We used to throw authorities off track by ditching the last leg of a trip. He's been threatening custody! I bet they planned to hitch to Howth, snatch Anya and disappear into the horizon. It makes sense now. That's why Vik arranged to get rid of my dad. He knew he could overtake my mom."

"They can't hurt your family from prison," Audra soothed, patting her shoulder.

"And *we* are the ones Paris-bound now!" Lee reminded. "We can arrange for your mom to meet us during the stopover or we can take the ferry from

France."

"Heck, we deserve to flit around the Eiffel Tower, don't ya think? I'll drop in on my old college roommate, and it's the City of Love, perfect for ya 'all!" Audra plucked Fitzy's I.D. from his hand.

"I thought it was the City of Lights?" Gal speculated, feeling calmer.

"It's whatever we want it to be." Lee's whisper brought back the Kryptonian chills that captivated her in the first place. "There's just one stipulation."

Galaxy braced herself, not sure what to expect. "Let me guess. We join the mile high club?"

"Hmmm, that does sound like us, but I was thinking, no cats!"

Chapter Twenty-One

Galaxy stumbled through the passenger tunnel in a groggy fog, clutching Lee's arm to steady herself. Landing in Collinstown at eight in the morning and their overnight flight had been useless. Whenever she'd close her eyes for more than twenty minutes, every shake and turbulent dip jolted her awake, comforted only when the morning aroma of coffee quilted the cabin.

"I slept fine," Audra announced, her usual perky self, as they emerged into the clamor of the airport hub. "Heck, I can snooze through hurricanes. In the Carolinas, we were raised to nestle into the hands of Jesus and batten down the hatches. Works wonders, Hon."

Gal clutched her sick stomach, envious.

"Thanks, I'll try anything at this point."

"I can sleep anywhere," Lee bragged, putting his arm around her. "But not when you're grabbing me every half hour."

"Guess I just can't keep my hands off you," she teased, embarrassed. He consoled her with a kiss.

Deep down, she wondered if her fitful slumber had more to do with the anxious anticipation of her daughter. Would she understand why she was away so long? Mum elected to ferry across Paris so they wouldn't have to hug and run, but she was eager to kiss that sweet face.

Before hitting the runway, Galaxy left resignation papers on Geoff's desk, thanking him for the opportunity. He had surprised the agents by acknowledging a job well done on the Fitzy case. And not only could Andle cook up great evidence in the lab, he was quite the cobbler, churning out alterations on their tickets, hot off the press!

Galaxy recalled his glumness when they exchanged hearty handshakes, his tight squeeze confirming Lee's prediction.

"Shall we grab some bangers before customs?" Lee yawned, spotting a café chalkboard, the crisp sizzle of meat awakening his senses.

"You two are relentless," Audra scoffed, shaking her head.

"He means sausages," Gal explained, as they headed over. "But I guess that doesn't plead our case very well, does it?"

Their chuckles were interrupted by the warning whirl of the baggage claim, startling them as they waited to cross the congested corridor. Only Galaxy glanced up, entranced by the spinning suitcases, now unfocused blobs of buckskin and canvas. Suddenly a huddled ball of black leather tumbled onto the conveyer belt, mutating into a craggy-faced human!

The dizzying hallucination felt like a werewolf movie in IMAX. "There's a bad guy riding the carousel," she panicked, pawing her partner.

"Let's get you a caffeine I.V. — Stat!" Lee laughed, leading her away. "Hopefully you can catch some Z's on the next flight."

She blinked, snapping herself out of the sluggish stupor, but the dream sequence didn't disappear. Instead, the disfigured chap with the ascot and greasy ponytail rolled off nonchalantly, blending into the bag-grabbing crowd before gimping away.

From The Author

I cherish my readers! If you enjoyed this book, please follow me on my author page at Amazon.com for new title announcements, interesting tidbits, and fun quizzes. Reviews are greatly appreciated and help boost ratings.

amazon.com/author/chelepedersensmith

Have a favorite character or scene? Drop me an email:

cpsmithbooks22@gmail.com

Galaxy O'Jordan was born in a 1981 journalism class at Colonial High School in Orlando, Florida. The challenge: develop a cast of characters and the last scene of a T.V. script, in which the teacher provided the premise—an assassination attempt on the Russian Premier.

Galaxy had a minor but similar role then of "honey trapping" an agent. I'm not sure where her name came from. I was going for something exotic, I'm sure. It's also quite possible, I was influenced by the hoopla of the first manned space shuttle launch Columbia that spring.

Flash forward to 2014: Galaxy is dusted off, dipped into the fountain of youth and begins a metamorphic journey, blossoming into a major complex character. It's been quite a joy ride!

I enjoy writing multi-genre stories, poems, and creative non-fiction.

As a hopeful romantic myself, love stories coupled with comedy and a little suspense are my favorite. Craving more Lee and Galaxy? A sequel is brewing as well as these upcoming titles.

The Pearly Gates Phone Company

Confessions of a Goody-Goody

Will the Real Green Phantom Please Stand Up?

If you've enjoyed Behind Frenemy Lines, here's a short satire I wrote for a creative writing workshop in February 2016. It's based on the painting, "Subway Entrance 1938", by Mark Rothko. I think you'll recognize a familiar character.

Time Hop

(The Epochracy Files)

Rooney McCallahan adjusted the fez cap that matched his crimson hair and as he trudged wearily down the subway steps that November first night in 1938, the weight of the world on his scrawny shoulders. Maybe not the whole world, but definitely the dizzying whirlwind of The Plaza Hotel where he carted suitcases and trunks for glamorous people who could very well carry their own baggage. It was honest work albeit heavy at times, especially when big families or starlets fumbled in with numerous sets.

He was an optical illusion: one hundred and forty pounds at five eleven but stronger and more muscular than he appeared. He really was nothing more than a mule, he often joked with his buddies down at Dempsey's Bar. At least the guests tipped well, he thought as he habitually patted his pocket, grateful to have a job in these times.

He was so deep in thought and exhausted; he didn't notice the smartly dressed woman in yellow ascending from the train pits as he stomped downstairs. Not that he would know who she was yet.

When she emerged from Grand Central Terminal to the noisy streets, she ducked under a candy-striped awning, glanced into her makeup mirror pretending to powder her nose and… waited.

Rooney reached the humid underworld otherwise known as the bowels of New York City. It was his usual shift, so he knew the routine by heart. He leaned against a pillar and gazed at his Bulova watch. It seemed out of place on his blue collar wrist, but it had been a gratuity from Doug Corrigan himself!

What luck to carry bags for "Wrong-Way" Corrigan, famous trans-Atlantic aviator who ended up in Dublin instead of California just a mere five months ago! The Joe was mocked for the mix-up, but it only made him more human, more lovable. He admired his moxie for owning it.

He sighed, shifting his weight. A rat scurried across the tracks, hauling debris between his teeth. He groaned instinctively, not at the scrounger, but at the idea of lifting one more thing that night. Crowds were thinning, but he caught breathy fragments as people darted past.

"—felt just like Fay Wray on top of the Empire State Building,"

"—the Rainbow Room is so keen,"

"I just love Broadway, don't you?"

He made a habit of eavesdropping. It

seemed everyone was doing exciting things with their existence and what was he doing? Living life vicariously through them, that's what! He never took a trip, had barely stepped out of Manhattan in all his twenty-five years, for crying out loud. But he lived in the Big Apple, where else did he need to go? Just in case, he'd been saving his tips in a jar, safely hidden inside the prohibition cabinet. It would do him good to get out of his rut.

As if the Universe agreed, a gap in the crowd revealed the rectangular corner of tattered leather peeking out from behind a beam. "I'm always seeing luggage," Roon sighed in exasperation, shaking his head and the urge to investigate. Big deal, someone set their attaché case down to read the paper. He saw it all the time. But when the new herd clambered aboard the subway, there it remained, unclaimed with some sort of aura around it, beckoning him like a beacon.

He sauntered over and inspected it. No one was in sight. "Odd," he mumbled, noncommittally flipping a tag over with his foot. No name, just a taunting, *"Do you accept this mission?"*

What did that mean? His curiosity began to spin tales. Nazi spy ring? The idea woke him up a bit. He always dreamed of espionage; he'd be good at it, too. After all, he heard millions of conversations and kept plenty of confidences at the hotel. Contemplating, this box held possibilities. Was it filled with a fortune? What if it was empty, just a trick? Or worse, an advertising gimmick? If it was truly something mystical, and how could that be since magic didn't exist, would there be no turning back if he unlatched it? It was a risky decision. True, he was tired of his humdrum life, but he wasn't ready to ditch it for the unknown on a moment's notice.

To put pressure on his overthinking, he heard the rail cars whooshing into the stop. It was now or never. He heard the sing-song ding of the open doors; he'd only have a few seconds to leap aboard if he wanted to go home. On the other hand, what if he grabbed the case and made a run for it? He could decide later, have a chance to pack.

Grasping the handle in a swift motion, he swung his arm in the direction of the train and made a mad dash. Except the briefcase didn't budge. It was heavy-bottomed as if a magnetic force was weighing it down. He fell flat on his back. The subway chugged away and gained speed. "Well, that's that," he muttered under his breath.

With the platform empty again, he looked around cautiously, held his breath and flicked the buckle with a snap. C-r-e-a-k...

Blinded by a brilliant glare, he was hurled through a vortex of swirling centuries as four digit numbers flew past him. He realized they were dates when he saw the passage of time rise and set on a Roman sundial and a giant sandglass spinning against the backdrop of Big Ben's hourly chimes.

Outside on the curb, the lady snapped her compact shut. Her work was done for today.

Rooney squinted at the harsh sun streaming through a window. Huddled in the corner of a room with a pounding headache, he tried propping himself up on an elbow.

"He's awake," a male voice called toward the door, then in his direction, "How are you feeling? You've been out awhile."

"Head hurts, light too bright," he mumbled. Did he have a seizure on the subway floor?

He forced an eye open to scan the drab surroundings of wall-to-wall filing cabinets. Patting the floor around him, he realized he was on a cot, then holding his throbbing brain, discovered his cap was missing. Great! They would dock his pay.

The tanned man with dark hair and devilish green eyes leaned against a desk, eating a sandwich. Rooney heard a rapid tapping of heels, and then a brisk blonde woman was flooding his face with a flashlight.

"Made it through the bridge just fine," was her verdict, lifting each eyelid.

"Hey lady, do ya mind! What's with all the bright light? Am I dead?"

When they didn't answer right away, he panicked. "I am, aren't I? Oh jeez, I never spent any of my tips or smooched Patty Marcus. I knew I shoulda went for it."

"Are you dizzy? Vertigo's often a side effect," the man informed, pen cap between his teeth as he scribbled on a clipboard.

"Side effect?" Rooney echoed, still not sure what was going on. "Of death?"

The female chimed in. "No, time-travel. Welcome to the FBI."

"T-Time travel? Yeah, good one. Another H.G. Wells scare?" he chortled. "Did Frankie put ya up to this? He's such a pranksta." The seriousness of the duo made Rooney nervous. "Did you say FBI? I coulda just took a train." They offered him a chair and a Dixie cup.

"Sure, if you came here in 1938. But you're in 2016." The man tossed this fact over his shoulder casually as Rooney swigged the water.

He choked mid-gulp and bolted up in a panic. With regained breath he sputtered, "Hell, two thousand—whoa, did you say *two thousand sixteen*? Nah, not possible, this is a dream, a mistake!" Did he really just leap through the sci-fi future?

Feeling trapped in a nightmare, he unbuttoned his uniform coat for air. "I musta hit my head at the station, I remember fallin'. Yeah, that's it!" He paced anxiously, tugging at his scarlet strands. "Wait a minute, I'm wisin' up now—you slipped me a micky, didn't ya?" He frantically checked his cash to make sure he wasn't robbed.

"Calm down and listen." The woman in yellow pointed to his seat, then added "please" almost sarcastically. "Does a briefcase at the subway platform ring a bell? Me, passing you on the stairwell?" She impatiently tapped her foot, waiting for it all to sink in.

Rooney rubbed the back of his freckled neck, deep in recall. *"Do you accept this mission"*? So that was you?"

"I'm Sunny D'Angelo, time-travel agent. I make sure the trip is smooth between jumps. This is Talon Smythe. He handles assignments and covert details."

"Yeah, right. I'm a G-Man, just like that!" he snorted. "You take anyone off the street, whoever opens the case?"

"You weren't random."

Sunny's gaze possessed an encyclopedia of knowledge. While his speech flat-lined, she gestured to his wrist. "You have the watch, right?"

"This? It was just a tip from—you mean..."

"Yep, he's a jumper. In fact, one of our best recruiters." She leaned against the metal cabinet and filed her nails.

Stunned, McCallahan wiped his sweaty palms on his pants. "So that's why it runs backward! I thought it was just a marketin' gag on ol' Corrigan. What's next--zigzaggin' 'round different zones luggin' that case?" He couldn't help show disappointment. So far, it wasn't very appealing.

"Well, dimensions," D'Angelo corrected, freshening her lipstick.

"Say, I'm just a crumb, I got no business bein' here." He stood, brushing them off. "Nice meetin' you guys, but I hafta make tracks." A few strides forward, he timidly retreated, finding their stance intimidating.

Intense frowns told him he didn't have a choice. Then it occurred to him he had no idea how to get home. "Say, I don't hafta shoot anyone, do I? Blood makes me queasy, and I never drilled a tommy gun."

"No violence," the assignment coordinator assured, holding the Top Secret portfolio. "And by the way, your watch is now activated as your transporter. Lightweight and more efficient."

That lifted Rooney's spirits, but he still didn't know much about the job. "Hey, wait. This ain't no trip for biscuits is it?" When they gave him blank stares, he added, "I'm gonna get paid, yeah?"

"Yes, you'll be compensated," Talon guaranteed, suppressing a chuckle.

"Just give him the folder, so he'll shut his trap already," Sunny interrupted as dancing illuminations transmitted from her compact. She dashed off to bait the next rookie.

"Here, very controversial so mum's the word! We need a troupe of time hoppers to intervene and prevent some faux pas. It's the Government's newest campaign for World Peace."

Rooney read the list. "*Conception Interception*? What the—Donald Trump, Hillary Clinton, Kanye West, 535 members of Congress? I don't understand. I never heard of any of these people."

"Exactly, and we'd like to keep it that way," Agent Smythe confirmed.

Made in the USA
Middletown, DE
24 February 2018